SERPENT GIRL

RAY GARTON

Chapter 1

I hadn't been to a carnival since I was a kid, but I'd just finished a job in Portland, and saw the sign as I passed south through the small northern California mountain town of Garver. I had nowhere to be, so I thought, *What the hell?* I was retired now, finally and for good. I'd done my last job. A stroll through a carnival seemed as good a way as any to celebrate my retirement.

When I was a teenager, I went to carnivals and amusement parks to meet girls. I had no such expectations now. I was forty-eight and intended to stay single. I had too much to hide to have a relationship.

I stopped at a little burger joint in town, got a burger and fries and a chocolate shake, waited for the evening to cool off a little. The late July heat in northern California was unbearable. Dark clouds gathered overhead, adding humidity to the heat.

It was getting dark by the time I finished eating, and I drove around until I found the fairgrounds. I saw the colorful Ferris Wheel and a couple of other rides towering in the distance and just followed them. I had to pay five bucks to park my freshly-washed Lexus in a dusty parking lot, then another five for admission at the front gate. I'd dropped ten bucks before I even got into the place. Carnivals had changed a lot. I remembered when you got in for nothing.

I lit a cigarette as I strolled down the midway. I felt overdressed in my grey slacks and a salmon-colored shirt with the long sleeves rolled up. Everyone else wore shorts, T-shirts or tank tops, sneakers or flip-flops.

I passed booths selling souvenirs and balloons and toys, small trailers selling greasy Chinese food, corn dogs, candied apples, funnel cakes, cotton candy, and even, of all things, deep-fried Twinkies. The deep-fried Twinkie vendors seemed to be very popular. No wonder America was such a fat nation—if people would eat deep-fried Twinkies, I could only assume they would eat *anything* as long as it had been dipped in hot grease first.

I stood for a while and watched a one-man band, gave a quarter to his little trained monkey. A bit farther up the midway, I veered off onto a well-tended lawn and sat on a bench in front of a gazebo stage where a ventriloquist was performing. I got a few chuckles from him and moved on, taking my time.

At the far end of the midway, there was a trailer selling beer. I tossed my cigarette onto the pavement, stamped it out with my shoe, then picked up the dead butt and dropped it in a garbage can. I walked down and got a large beer and sipped from it as I headed for the carnival grounds.

The first thing that caught my eye was the House of Terror. The haunted house attraction had always been a favorite of mine as a boy. This was the kind you rode through in a little cart. I bought my ticket from a skinny, filthy, toothless man in a little booth. The ticket was labeled Dupree Amusements. I'd seen the name on the sign over the front gate—Dupree Amusements, Inc.

I settled into a black cart that had red paint dribbling down from the edges like blood. The double-door entrance to the House of Terror sported a painting of zombies crawling out of their graves. But the paint had peeled badly, and the zombies were missing things like arms, legs or heads because they had peeled away. It was only a matter of time before the zombies disappeared altogether.

The cart followed the track and went through the double doors and into the dark.

They were always dark, the carnival haunted houses. But I remembered the ones I'd ridden and walked through as a boy, and there were always things jumping out of the darkness at me back then, and it always scared the hell out of me. I didn't let my friends know, of course, and I fought not to cry out when one of the pop-up creatures caught me off guard.

The first thing that popped out at me as I rode through the House of Terror that hot July evening was a metal dowel on a swivel. The dowel had bits of white fuzz attached to it, along with a single shard of plastic. The rest of it, whatever it had been, had broken off.

It was like that all the way through—empty metal dowels that swung out of the dark at me, the scares that once had been perched on them long broken off. Near the end, a pair of pale green hands that, at one time, might have glowed in the dark, reached out at me, but all the plastic fingers had been broken off.

As the light at the end of the tunnel neared, I thought, *Just like my childhood. All gone.*

I took my beer with me and walked away from the House of Terror feeling disappointed and a little sad.

I thought a ride on the Ferris wheel might cheer me up, so I bought a ticket and got on. It stopped while I was at the top. I sipped my beer as I took in the bird's-eye view of the carnival, which was colorful and festive. The sounds of laughter rose from below, babies cried and children shouted at each other. The mixed aromas of all the foods and the stinging exhaust from the rides wafted up to my car and filled my nostrils. You couldn't see the filthy, toothless ticket-sellers or the peeling paint. From up there, it all looked beautiful. Like an old street whore seen from a distance in the dark.

After that, I tossed the remainder of my beer into a garbage can—it was very weak, watery beer—and got on a small roller coaster. I decided carnival rides simply weren't as enjoyable as they'd been when I was a boy. They were also no fun alone. I remembered going to Coney Island with friends and riding dizzying rides until we got sick and couldn't stand up.

I paid fifty cents to see the World's Biggest Hog. It was big all right—*monstrous*—but, in the end, it was just a hog. I spent another fifty cents to see the World's Smallest Horse. That was more interesting. It was an American toy horse, and that's exactly what it looked like—*a toy*, but a living, breathing toy that got a lot of *awws* from the crowd. It made me smile.

I wandered around the carnival, played a couple of games. I threw darts at balloons, and when I won a small stuffed rabbit, I handed it to a little girl standing nearby, then returned her smile.

I took a handkerchief from my back pocket and dabbed my sweaty face, the back of my neck. Some sweat had gotten in my eye and stung. It was a hot, muggy night. I looked around, trying to decide where to go next.
A garish tent at the rear of the carnival grounds caught my eye. A chubby, snaggle-toothed barker stood out front and talked into a bullhorn. Behind him, the front of the tent was colorfully painted. A girl wrapped in snakes stood on one side, with lots of writing on the other:

SEE THE SERPENT GIRL!
WATCH HER COMMUNE WITH THE SNAKES!
SEE HER TAME THE SERPENT
THAT ONCE TEMPTED MAN!

The barker shouted through the bullhorn: "She speaks with them, ladies and gentlemen! She has a psychic connection to these ancient serpents! She has stunned the audiences of Europe, and now she's here to perform for you! Come see the Serpent Girl! Another show coming up, you don't wanna miss it! The Serpent Girl, ladies and gentlemen."

I went to the booth and bought a ticket, then went through the tent's entrance.

About twenty folding chairs were set up in two columns. A few men were already seated. Up front was an empty stage. There were speakers in the four corners of the tent.

I went to the front row and sat on the aisle.

A few minutes later, after a couple more men had come in, the lights in the tent went low. A man's voice came over the speakers: "Now, direct from the capitals of Europe to perform for you here tonight—Elise, the Serpent Girl!"

Music came up and a spotlight lit the center of the stage. She stepped into the light and began to dance in a tiny black, bejeweled bikini. In her arms, she held an enormous boa constrictor. She stroked the snake as she undulated to the music, then put it over her head and across her shoulders. The snake slowly began to coil around her as she danced.

Some of the men in the tent applauded.

One of them shouted, "Take it off, honey!"

She wasn't a terribly good dancer. By the time she held two snakes, she'd gone through all her moves and was just repeating herself.

But she was beautiful and I couldn't take my eyes off her.

Her skin was pale, her long, thick hair a deep red. She had strikingly full lips. She was voluptuous and filled the small bikini to its limit. At one point, she got down on all fours and crawled toward the front of the stage, three snakes wrapped around her, hair draped over half her face, Veronica Lake-style. Her lack of talent made little difference. Her bright blue eyes met mine a number of times, and each time, I felt a pleasant chill.

The men in the tent hooted and whistled. I watched silently, and wondered if Elise was her real name.

The show was short. A man came in and cleared out the tent, telling everyone it was over.

I stepped outside and lit a cigarette. I stood there a little while, looking around, wondering what to do next. I decided it would probably be best if I just got back in the car and hit the road again. There were a lot of miles to cover between Garver and Los Angeles. I didn't mind driving at night. In such heat, I preferred it.

I started to walk away from the tent when a woman screamed nearby, then said, rather loudly, "What did I tell you, huh? Didn't I say you ever touch me again, I'll *kill* you? Huh? *Didn't* I?"

I stopped and turned in the direction from which the scream had come, and realized it had sounded from behind the Serpent Girl tent. As I jogged along the side of the tent, I heard more.

"You cunt," a man said. "I was the best you ever had and you know it."

"The best?" the woman said with a gasp. "You're *scum*. I told you, we're over, we've *been* over. The *best*! What a laugh *that* is." She tipped her head back and barked a few harsh laughs. "You couldn't even—"

A sharp slap sounded an instant before I rounded the corner of the tent.

A tall, bear-like man in his fifties stood before the Serpent Girl, still in her sparkly, rhinestone bikini. He towered over her as he shook her hard by her shoulders, growling through clenched teeth, "You miserable bitch, you've always been worthless, and you'll always *be* worthless. You're crazier than a shit-house rat, and I hope you—"

"Hey," I said, "leave her alone."

"This is none a your fuckin' bidness, buddy," the big man said. He was bald on top, and the rusty ring of hair that went around from ear to ear was wildly mussed. "She belongs to me, I *own* her, and I'll—"

"Nobody owns me, you fat eunuch," she said. She spat the words.

He slapped her back-handed and knocked her down.

I stepped toward him and, without saying another word, punched him in the face. I caught him off guard and he almost went down, but not quite. As he raised a fist, I hit him again. He was big, but he was slow.

He collapsed to the grass and blood ran from his nose and over his mouth and chin. I watched him a moment until I was satisfied that the man was unconscious.

The Serpent Girl got to her feet, one hand pressed to the side of her face that had been slapped.

"You okay?" I said.

She set her jaw, stepped over to the man, and kicked him in the stomach. He curled up, almost in a ball, as he made a retching sound.

I took her elbow and pulled her back. "Don't do that, okay? He's fine, he's not getting up right away. And if he does," I added, hoping he'd hear, "I'll knock him down again."

She sighed. "I'm unemployed."

"What do you mean?" I said.

"He's my boss."

"Oh. I hope I didn't get you into any trouble."

"I was already in trouble."

"Anything I can do?"

"I don't know. You gotta car?"

"Where you headed?"

She jerked her head and said, "Come with me to my trailer. I wanna get the hell outta here before he gets his shit together."

I went with her toward a few rows of small trailers parked behind the tent. Hers was in the front row, third from the left, tan with a broad brown horizontal stripe. She opened the door and stepped up and in, turned on a light.

"C'mon inside," she said.

I joined her and pulled the door closed behind me.

"Have a seat," she said.

I sat at a table, which was set up like a booth in a diner, while she started putting things into a suitcase on the table in front of me. I looked around. Clothes and underwear were everywhere, as well as junk food wrappers and paper plates, an open bag of potato chips, boxes of various kinds of crackers and cookies. There was a pizza box with its lid up on the counter in the kitchenette. It contained three slices, curled with age, probably hard as rocks.

"Sorry for the mess," she said. "I'm not in here all that much when we're set up, so I haven't bothered to keep it neat and tidy."

I shrugged. "Just looks lived in."

"That's very nice of you, but really, it's a terrible mess," she said. "What's your name?"

"Steven. Benedetti."

"Italian, huh?"

I shrugged. "On my dad's side. You're Elise?"

"Nah, that's just showbiz. My name's Carmen Mattox."

"Where you headed, Carmen?"

"I got a sister in Sacramento. Haven't seen her in a long time. I'd like to go there. But I suppose you're not headed that way. You live around here?"

"No, I don't. As a matter of fact, I'm on my way to Los Angeles."

"Really? Then it's on your way." She turned to face me and said, "Look, I got money. I'll pay for half the gas."

I thought about it a moment as I watched her continue packing. I wasn't sure I wanted a passenger. On the other hand, if I was going to have a passenger, it might as well be a woman who looked like Carmen.

"Okay," I said.

She came to me, put a hand on each side of my face and gave me a generous kiss on the mouth. I was aware of her breasts pressing warmly against me as she said, "Thank you *so* much, I appreciate this *so* much. Let me put on some clothes."

She went to the back of the trailer, unfastening her bra on the way. In the back room, she turned on a light but did not close the door. From where I sat, I could see her as she changed. I watched her. That was what she wanted me to do.

She kept her back to me most of the time. Her ass was tight and curvaceous. Her breasts swayed heavily as she moved. She came back out wearing a tight red shirt that only came to the top of her belly, a pair of denim cut-offs, and red sneakers. I noticed she chewed her fingernails and barely had any left. She picked up her suitcase and smiled at me as she brushed some hair back out of her eyes with her fingers.

"Let's go," she said.

I got up and went to the door first and opened it.

The man who had slapped her around earlier stood just outside. Blood dribbled from his nose and cut lip, and his left eye was swollen.

"You're a glutton for punishment," I said.

"Look," he said, "this is none a your fuckin' bidness, and I'd 'preciate it if you'd just get the hell outta my way." When he saw Carmen behind me, he pointed at her and said, "You're *fired*, you hear me? And I *mean* it this time. I want you outta here in an *hour* or I'll call the cops. And you wouldn't want *that*, would you? No, you sure as hell wouldn't want *that*, honey."

Carmen stepped around me and left the trailer. "You can't fire me, I *quit!*"

"What else you gonna do?" he shouted, fists clenched at his sides.

"Anything's better than working for you, Lenny."

I stepped down and took her elbow. "Come on, let's go."

"Yeah, that's right," Lenny said. "Hook up with the first sucker who comes along."

"Let's just go," I said.

Lenny lunged forward, a fist raised to strike her. I slammed my body into his and knocked him backward. Then I stepped back, swung my foot up, and kicked the big man in the nuts. Lenny doubled over, then fell to the ground with a long groan. As he vomited, Carmen and I turned and walked away.

Several seconds later, Lenny managed to shout, in a cracked voice, "You're...gonna be...*sorry!*"

I released a single chuckle. "He says you're going to be sorry."

"I think he was talking to you," Carmen said with a smile. "Where are you parked?"

"In that dust bowl of a parking lot out front. For five lousy bucks."

"What kinda car you got?"

"A Lexus."

"A Lexus, huh? That's nice."

We talked as we walked across the carnival grounds, down the Midway, and to the front gate.

"Oh, damn," Carmen said just inside the gate.

"What's wrong?"

"I left my purse in the trailer."

"Well, let's go back and—"

"No," she said. "Wait right here. I'll run and get it."

"I'm not sure that's a good idea," I said, thinking of Lenny, who was probably very pissed off at the moment.

"I'll be fine. I'm just gonna run in and grab it and come right back." She pointed to a nearby trailer selling soft-serve cones. "Get an ice cream, and by the time you're done with it, I'll be back."

She was lithe and swift and she disappeared into the crowd quickly. I went over to the trailer and bought a chocolate cone. The ice cream began to melt immediately in the wilting heat and I licked furiously to catch the dribbles down the side. I had to eat it quickly before it completely liquefied. I grabbed two napkins from the dispenser in the trailer window and wiped my mouth when I was finished. Then I ate the cone. Carmen had not returned.

I paced a little just inside the front gate, people coming and going all around me. I didn't look at my watch but I waited long enough to start worrying. I was considering going to check on her when Carmen arrived with her purse slung over her shoulder. She walked with a limp.

"What happened?" I said. "Are you all right?"

"Yeah, I just twisted my ankle a little comin' outta the trailer," she said. "I didn't even see Lenny. I don't know where he was."

"You want to wait here while I get the car?"

She shook her head. "Oh, no, I'm fine, really. Walking's probably the best thing for it."

"Okay, if you say so."

We walked along a row of cars. Mine was up ahead.

"Where you from?" she said.

"Originally? New Jersey."

"I'm from Iowa." She laughed. "I ran away with the carnival when I was seventeen. I been dropping in and out of it ever since."

"How long ago was that?"

She raised one brow as she looked at me. "That a round-about way of asking me how old I am?"

I returned to her smile. "Something like that."

"I'm legal, that's all you gotta know," she said with a smirk. "I haven't been a minor in a long time. Even when I *was* a minor, I wasn't a minor. Not really."

"Tough home life?"

"Oh, it sucked. Trust me."

We got to the car.

"Nice wheels," she said.

"It's filthy now," I said. I unlocked the doors and opened hers for her.

"A gentleman," she said. "That's a rare find these days."

"I took a course online."

Once in the car, I started the engine.

"What do you do?" she said.

"I'm retired."

"Really? You look a little young to retire."

"It was a stressful job."

"Doing what?" she said.

It had taken a little longer than usual, but it was time to start lying. "I was a consultant," I said.

"A *consultant*? What does that mean?"

"That means I traveled around the country helping businesses set up or repair computer networks."

"Doesn't sound so stressful."

"Ever dealt with a man whose entire network has been down for three days? It's hazardous work."

She took a cigarette and lighter from her purse. "You mind if I smoke in here?"

"Nope."

She lit up and rolled her window down halfway. "It's starting to cool a little, I think."

"Not enough for me," I said.

I drove through Garver and got on Interstate 5. It was ten-eighteen by the clock in my dash.

Carmen leaned her head back on the rest and closed her eyes.

"Tired?" I said.

"Exhausted, is all."

"Feel free to sleep. The seat goes back if you want to stretch out."

"You're gonna drive all the way to Sacramento tonight?" She lifted her head and turned to me. "I mean, you're not gonna stop for the night?"

"I wasn't planning on it, no. Why?"

"Mm. Well, a bed sounds real good tonight. Maybe a hot bath. I've got money for my own room. Unless you had other plans."

"Other plans, huh?" It was my turn to smirk.

She smiled as she turned her eyes front. "Got any music?"

"Nothing new. Some jazz. Some rock from the Sixties and Seventies. Some scattered pop."

"Jazz sounds nice."

I turned on the CD player, and a moment later, Miles Davis began to play. Later, while Carmen slept, I listened to some early Steely Dan for a while.

I looked over at Carmen. She was lovely at rest. She lay back in the seat with her left forearm across her eyes. Her lifted arm stretched the bellyshirt up on that side and revealed the vanilla scoop of the underside of her breast. A strip of creamy belly was visible from the bottom of the shirt to the top of the cut-offs. Tattooed wings, like angel wings, spread out on each side of her navel. Her shoes were on the floor, left leg flat, but her right foot was up on the seat, with her knee bent high. She had long legs that tapered nicely.

I couldn't pin down her age, but she was somewhere in her thirties. Her mileage showed a little better up close, but it wasn't unflattering on her.

She had a spark in her, there was no question about that. If I hadn't kicked Lenny in the nuts first, I have no doubt she would have gotten around to it eventually. She was as crusty as she needed to be. Apparently, growing up had not been a pleasant experience for her.

Was it ever a pleasant experience for *anyone*?

I found myself wondering about her relationship with Lenny. And what it would be like to kiss those bee-stung lips. I wondered what her hair smelled like.

I took a deep breath and shook my head. "I need a break," I muttered.

"Huh?" Carmen said as she sat up. She looked around with half-closed eyes.

"I was just talking to myself," I said.

"How long've I been sleeping?"

"A little over three hours."

"No shit?"

"I shit you not."

She sniffed as she leaned forward and put her face in her hands a moment. Then she scrubbed her hands up and down a couple of times and sat up again, adjusted the seat. She lit a cigarette. "I sure could use some coffee," she said. "Better yet, some scotch. Glenfiddich."

"Your favorite?"

"Yep. I gotta lotta favorites." She laughed playfully. "You'd probably be shocked by a few of my favorite things."

"The song?" I said. "Please don't sing it. I hate *The Sound of Music.*"

She laughed. "That was accidental, by the way—but I *love* that movie. *The Sound of Music.* I watched it once when I was a little girl. Mom watched it with me, and it was one of the few times I remember her bein' sober. She, you know, she enjoyed it—the movie, I mean—but..." Creases appeared above Carmen's huddled eyebrows. "...she was shakin', I remember. Her hands shook real bad. But she sat through the whole movie with me. She didn't get up and make herself a drink. Of course, soon as the movie was over, she was headin' for the kitchen. But it was nice while it lasted. Yeah, I remember really loving that movie."

"Your mother was an alcoholic?" I said.

"Oh, yeah."

"Well, I hope you understand what a sacrifice that was for her," I said. "Do you have any idea how hard it was for her to sit through that movie for three hours or so, listening to those songs, without getting up to make herself a drink? I mean, that would be difficult even for someone who *wasn't* an alcoholic. That was...it was a gift from her, sitting through that movie sober with you."

She nodded. "Yeah, I thought of that. But only recently. Wish I'd realized that back then. Mostly...I just always wished she coulda stopped drinking. Or had never had me in the first place. One or the other. She tried to quit the bottle a couple times, but she couldn't take the withdrawals. And she wouldn't let us take her to the hospital. I 'member this one time, she threw up all over the living room. She was shakin' so bad, she wet herself. It was—" She shook her head. "God, it was awful. It was the last time she tried to stop. Far as I know, anyway. Like I said, I ran off with the carnival when I was seventeen. Well, actually, I ran off with a boy *in* the carnival. But that's a different story."

"What about your father?"

She made an *ugh* sound. "He was more interested in me than he was in his wife. Of course, Mom was drunk all the time."

"Do you think it's possible that she drank to numb and blind herself to what was going on between your father and you?" I said.

Carmen turned to me slowly. "What're you, a shrink?"

I chuckled. "No."

Her brow was wrinkled again. "What does some computer consultant know about analyzin' somebody's head he never met? Huh?"

I shrugged. "Sorry. I didn't mean to offend."

She sighed and faced front again, leaned her head back. "I really need to stop soon. I gotta pee. And I'm hungry. And I wanna sleep in a real bed. Let's stop at a motel, okay? Please?"

I thought about it, checked the time. It was two-twelve in the morning. We were only a little more than an hour away from Sacramento, but I realized I was getting tired myself. I nodded and said, "Yeah. Okay."

A few miles later, we came to a truck-stop with a diner and bar called Pantyhose Junction. Across the street from it was a motel.

When I took the turn-off, she said, "Thanks, Benedetti. I'm starvin'. I hope they serve a good steak here."

I looked at her. "You don't strike me as a steak-eater."

"Oh, honey, when it comes to a good steak, I can eat most men under the table."

"How do you keep your girlish figure?"

"By only doing it once or twice a year."

I turned left at the stop sign and crossed the freeway on the overpass.

Chapter 2

We went to the Pantyhose Junction first. To get to the diner, we had to go through the gift shop. It sold knick-knacks, batteries, flashlights, cold drinks, paperbacks, magazines, candy bars, a little of everything. There were glossy burlwood clocks on all the walls and each one bore an image—Elvis in all his stages of life, Jesus on the cross, Jesus with children, and there were a few with Jesus and Elvis shaking hands.

There were more clocks on the walls in the diner, all for sale: John Wayne in a cowboy hat, Ronald Reagan in a cowboy hat, George W. Bush in a cowboy hat, Jesus *and* George W. Bush, hat not included, and Johnny Cash.

The hostess was a perky young thing and she escorted us to our booth, where she presented us with menus and assured us our waitress would be along in a moment.

Our waitress was, according to her nameplate, Greta, a pear-shaped woman in her fifties who apparently was forced by her employers to wear a hideous pink uniform with a short-short skirt and pantyhose, like all the other waitresses. I felt sorry for Greta, because I was sure she knew as well as anyone that she had no business in such an outfit, but she was probably divorced and had raised her kids on a couple of waitressing jobs at a time, because out there in the middle of nowhere, what else was there for her to do? And now, in her fifties, it was all she could do because it was all she'd ever known. And yet her face opened into a jolly grin when she came to our table and produced her order pad and a pen.

"Can I get you folks a cocktail tonight?" she said.

Carmen said, "I'd like a double scotch on the rocks. And a cup of coffee. And put this on separate checks."

Greta stopped writing and said, "You want the scotch and the coffee…together?"

She nodded. "I need the caffeine. I'm having a caffeine headache."

"Oh, I've had those, honey," Greta said. "They're awful. Double scotch, rocks, and a cuppa java coming up." She turned to me as she flipped the page in her tablet.

"I'd like a vodka stinger, please," I said.

For dinner, Carmen ordered a rib-eye, rare, with a salad, a baked potato with all the toppings, and cheesecake afterward. I ordered fish and chips.

Our cocktails came and I sipped mine. Carmen took two big swallows of hers, then sipped her coffee.

"Whatever became of your father?" I asked.

"Who knows?" she said with a shrug. "Once I left home, I never looked back. Last I heard from my cousin Naomi—the only relative I have anything to do with at all, and not very often—she told me Mom died of liver failure, but that Dad was still alive and well."

"I'm sorry about your mother."

"Yeah, and I'm sorry about my father. It took a long time for me to forgive Mom for dying and leaving me so…I don't know, so alone, even though I hadn't seen her in so many years. If that makes any sense."

"It does."

"Dad was a plumber. He was well-known in the community for being an honest, fair businessman. He was a member of the Elks Lodge and the Rotary Club. He was a church deacon, always involved in charitable activities. Everybody thought he was a great guy."

I nodded. "Typical. The worst monsters are the ones right under your nose. In church or in school. Or right next door. They know how to keep themselves hidden in plain sight. No one knows until someone either talks or accidentally discovers them." I realized Carmen was giving me a strange look. "Why are you looking at me like that?" I said.

"You sure you're just some computer consultant?" she said.

"I'm afraid so."

"You talk like you're…I don't know, a writer or somethin'. Or a cop. Are you one of them cops who writes books about cops?"

"No, I'm not a cop. I've done a little writing. Just as an outlet. Nothing professional. I've thought about trying my hand at fiction."

She stared across the table at me for a while, like a cat staring at a mouse-hole. She took a couple more swallows of her scotch, then decided to finish it with a flip of her head. Finally, she said, "I don't think you're a computer programmer."

"Consultant," I said.

"Whatever. That's not what you are."

"What makes you say that?"

Her breasts swayed a bit when she shrugged. "I dunno. Can't put my finger on it. I think it's your eyes. You got real serious eyes. Too serious to be a computer man."

"I'm afraid I'm pretty boring."

She grinned and shook her head. "No. There's nothing boring about those eyes."

Greta came with our orders and we began to eat.

"What's your story?" she said.

"I don't have much of one. I had an uneventful childhood. I got good grades in school. Went to college to see what *they* were up to. And I've worked in computers all my adult life. That's about it."

Her eyes narrowed a little as she looked at me with suspicion, trying to stifle a smile. "It's gonna take a while to figure you out, huh?"

I shrugged again and said, "Nothing to figure out."

"What're you gonna write about?"

"I don't know. I thought a thriller, maybe. A novel. You know, crime fiction of some kind, maybe a mystery."

"That'd be cool. I never knew anybody wrote a book before."

"I haven't even started it yet," I said. "It's just something I've thought about doing."

"Any brothers and sisters?"

"No. An only child."

"Really? My older sister and I always fought when we were kids. What was it like being the only one?"

I shrugged again. "I don't know. I have nothing to compare it to. It was fine, really. My parents were good to me. My dad whipped me with his belt when I did something really stupid or destructive, but that only happened a few times. I was a pretty good kid. See? I was boring even back then."

Carmen chewed on a piece of steak and waited for me to go on.

"What about Lenny?" I said. "How'd you get involved with him?"

She swallowed her food and said, "How does anybody get involved with anybody? I should've left him a long time ago."

"How long were you involved?"

"You sure you're not planning to write a book about *me*?"

"Sorry. I didn't mean to pry. I'm not nosy, really. Just curious."

She took another bite of food, but watched me as she ate. She took the napkin from the table, unfolded it and wiped her mouth, then put it in her lap. "Almost six years," she said. "Can you believe it? Well, that's not really true. It was off and on over that time. Don't ask me why I ever went back to him. But as much of an asshole as he always was, he didn't start hittin' me until recently. The last five, six months. That's it for me. The hittin', I mean. I can put up with a lotta shit from a guy, but if he starts hittin' me, all bets are off."

I nodded as I dipped a French fry into a small puddle of ketchup, then popped it into my mouth. "Funny how bad relationships always seem to be a lot harder to get out of and away from than the good ones, huh?"

"Ain't that the truth," she said as she cut into her steak.

I finished my fish and chips and ordered a slice of apple pie *a la mode* when Greta came for my plate.

Not long after that, Carmen ate the last of her steak, potato, and salad. Greta came and took Carmen's plate, too.

After our dessert came, Carmen said, "So, we gonna get one room or two tonight?"

I smiled at her.

She shrugged. "Somebody had to bring it up."

"One room."

She smiled then, and it was a beautiful thing.

I had to take a leak, so I excused myself and went through the gift shop to the restroom in the front hall, near the entrance to the bar. As I stood at the urinal, I wondered if I was making a mistake. It was only one night. She was going to Sacramento and I to Los Angeles. In a week or so, I planned to go to the Caribbean and spend some time doing nothing but reading on the beach. I had some condoms in the glovebox of the car—never knew when they would come in handy.

I flushed the urinal and washed my hands at the sink with the *faux* marble countertop, dried my hands on paper towels.

When I headed back out to the table, I saw a man tugging on Carmen's arm, trying to pull her out of the booth. He had grey hair and wore a green plaid shirt under a pair of overalls.

"Get your filthy hands off me or I'll *kill* you," Carmen said.

He was smiling and swaying.

I rushed up to the man, took his free hand and squeezed on a spot that's excruciatingly painful when squeezed hard. The man's knees bent and he let go of Carmen, grabbed my arm and squeezed as his mouth dropped open and his eyes bulged.

"I'm going to let you go," I said quietly to the drunk man, "and you're going to quietly leave, all right?"

He made a small sound in his throat as he nodded.

I dropped his hand and he clutched it with the other as he straightened up. He stepped around me, a little unsteadily, and made his way back through the gift shop.

"I hope you didn't know him," I said.

She looked like I'd just stepped on her foot. "No. I've never seen him before. He's a trucker."

"How do you know?"

"He wanted me to go out to his truck and get in with him." She made a disgusted face. "Like I'm some kinda lot lizard."

"What's a lot lizard?"

"A truck stop hooker," she said. "You never heard of lot lizards?"

I shook my head no. "Learn something new every day."

"Now I gotta go to the little girl's room." She stood and left the table.

As I sat there and waited, Greta brought our check. A few minutes later, Carmen returned to the table and we went to the register in front to pay our bill. I left a hefty tip for Greta.

When we got outside, it was raining a hot, sticky rain. We got soaked hurrying back to the car. Once inside, she said, "We gotta get a room with a tub. I gotta take a nice hot bath."

"Sounds good," I said as I pulled out of the parking lot onto the road. I went a few yards up and turned left into the motel. Under the portico in front of the office, I stopped the car and told her I'd only be a minute. There was no one at the desk, but I could hear a television going in the back room. I rang the bell on the desk.

A small man, Indian or Pakistani, came out and smiled at me.

I said, "I'd like a room with a king-size bed and a bathtub."

"King and bath." He told me the price, and I paid cash. I signed the register book as Mr. & Mrs. Paul Griffin of Honeoye, NY. "Number one-nineteen. In the back." He handed me the key on a diamond-shaped piece of plastic labeled 19.

I got back in the car and drove over to one-nineteen, which was on the ground floor of the two-level complex.

"Did you get a tub?" she said.

"I got a tub."

"Goodie," she said. She surprised me when she leaned over and kissed my cheek.

I carried our suitcases, one each, into the room and put them on the bed. I'd grabbed the package of condoms from the car's glovebox and slipped it into my pocket.

Inside, Carmen tossed her purse onto the bed and went straight to the bathroom.

I turned on the bedside lamp, then the dark-brown swamp cooler in a small window in the back of the room.

"Well, it's not very big," she said from the bathroom, "but I think it'll hold both of us, if we, uh, y'know, cuddle."

I smiled.

She started the bath running. When she came out of the bathroom, she was naked. My breath caught in my throat for a moment.

"You're too slow," she said.

I just stood there and stared at her for several seconds, took her in. She was stunning. I smiled as my eyes moved over her. She smiled back, standing there while I admired her. It was obviously something Carmen was good at, being admired. I started to undress as she went to the nightstand on one side of the bed and turned on a clock-radio that was bolted down. She turned the dial until she found Joan Jett singing "I Love Rock and Roll," and she turned up the volume a little.

"I like this song," she said as she turned to me.

I stepped out of my pants and carefully hung them up in the small open closet near the door, then did the same with my shirt. When I turned around, she was standing by the bed with her hands on her hips, staring at me.

"You've got a nice body, Benedetti," she said.

I smiled. "And you have…a *beautiful* body."

She did. It was curvy and soft, but nicely toned, pale, freckled here and there. Her nipples were rosy and puffy, my favorite kind. She came to me after I took off my boxers, put her arms around me. I kissed her and our lips melted together. Her kiss was needy and strong, and she clutched at my back with her fingers. Her breasts pressed to me as I moved my hands over her smooth back, down to her ass. Her skin was like silk and I squeezed her cheek with my right hand.

She pulled back a little and gulped a breath, then grinned. It was a charming look that said, Well, that was fun!

"You an ass man or a tit man, Benedetti?" she said through a smile.

"I'm a breast man," I said, "but I have an intense appreciation for the entire package."

"What is it with men and tits?" she said as she reached down and fondled me.

I scooped a hand under her left breast and lifted it to my lips to kiss the nipple, which quickly hardened and grew under my lips in that way only puffy nipples do.

"If I knew that," I said, "I'd probably have my own TV show."

She laughed.

Carmen was right, the tub wasn't very big. We managed to squeeze into it, facing each other, our knees up, pressed tightly together in the hot water.

"We need some bubbles and candles," she said.

She got up and turned around, sat down between my legs with her back to me. I got the bar of soap from the corner of the tub, unwrapped it, tossed the wrapper to the floor. I dipped the soap in the water and rubbed it over her breasts, lathered them up and then rubbed my hands slowly over them. They were magnificent.

"I don't mind when you stare at them," she said.

"What?"

"They get stared at a lot. They're not *huge*, but they're um…well, I don't know, they're—"

"They're perfect," I said.

She laughed. "Okay, they're perfect. I get tired of people staring at them. But when you stare at them…I don't mind."

"You caught me, huh?"

A single laugh through her nose. "Yes."

"I thought I was being so cool, so nonchalant."

"Nah, can't fool me. I know when you're lookin' at 'em. I can *feel* it when someone's lookin' at 'em."

"They should be displayed in a museum."

"Oh? And what would I do for tits then?"

"Your whole body should be in a museum."

We were silent for a while. Journey played on the radio in the other room. Apparently, Carmen had found an eighties station.

I slipped one hand down between her legs and found that she was smooth, completely hairless.

Then she put her hand over mine on her breast and stroked it with her thumb, whispered, "It's been a while since somebody said something nice to me. Thank you."

"Then it's high time," I said. I bent my head down and kissed her neck, smelled her hair. I couldn't place the perfume, and it wasn't very strong, but it was musky and stirring. I nibbled on her ear as she reached back and found me, stroked me.

We eventually stood up in the tub and took a quick shower together as it drained, washed each other's hair. We gave our bodies a cursory drying with the towels and went to the bed. She pulled the covers back, and we got in. She reached over and turned off the bedside lamp while I put on a condom.

She spread her legs and I settled in between them. She reached down, rubbed the head of my penis up and down between her lips, then directed me in.

Carmen never held still beneath me. She moved constantly. She thrust her hips up to meet me each time I plunged into her.

She laughed in the middle of it. It was a joyful laugh, and it made me smile down at her. She dug her nailless fingertips into my back, her heels into my ass, and used her legs to pull me into her with each upward thrust of her hips.

We fell into a good rhythm and she laughed again.

"Roll over, roll over," she breathed urgently.

We rolled over and she smiled down at me, her hair hanging down in wet strands. She moved on me in ways no woman ever had. She bent down and let her breasts smack me in the face as they lolled back and forth.

Headlights passed over the room's front windows. Even though the blinds were closed, light seeped through them and around them, and stripes of it moved over us, giving me a second's glimpse of her wide-eyed, open-mouthed face.

"Oh, yeah!" she cried, sitting up again. "Yeah, you're doin' it to me, you're doin' it to me." She went wild on me as she cried out again and again.

Someone in the next room pounded on the wall behind the bed.

She laughed again, and that made me laugh, and when I came, I propped myself up on one elbow and held her to me tightly as she continued to move on me.

Our movements gradually slowed down. Sweat trickled down my forehead and temples.

She rolled off me as I sighed. I expected her to lie in the crook of my arm, but instead, she went down, took the condom off my penis, and took me in her mouth.

"Oh, god," I breathed.

I wasn't ready to go again, but she didn't seem to mind. She devoured me, and a lot sooner than I expected, I was hard again. She continued to suck on me as she cupped my balls in her hand. She was alive down there, going at it. I'd never had a blowjob like it before in my life, and I wanted it to go on, but she got me off. She kept me in her mouth the whole time and gulped furiously at the end.

Afterward, she rested her head on my chest. "Got your heart pumping pretty fast, didn't I?"

I wiped a hand down my sweaty face. "You've got everything pumping pretty fast, Carmen. That was...it was...incredible. I'm...in awe. I'm not even sure exactly what it was you were *doing* down there, but it was...spectacular."

She lifted her head and looked at me, our faces inches apart. "I've never gotten any complaints."

"What brought all this on?" I said. "I thought this was going to be nothing more than a simple drive to Sacramento."

"I thought you woulda guessed by now," she said. "I got a thing for older men."

"Ah. I see."

"You're pretty hot for an older guy, Benedetti. How old are you?"

"I'll be fifty-two in November."

"Mm, not so old. Only twenty years older than me, that's not such a big deal. It's the grey in your hair that gives you away. Nothing else."

I tipped my head up and kissed her. She scooted up and curled a long leg over me.

I said, "You have the body of a twenty-year-old."

"Well, I think it's been a while since you seen a naked twenty-year-old, you wanna know the truth, Benedetti. But I appreciate the compliment."

"And you have the face of...I don't know, like I dreamed you."

"You're sweet. You don't come off sweet at first, you know. You come off...I don't know, kinda stand-offish, maybe a tough guy."

"A tough guy, huh?"

"Well, maybe. Like you could be if you're pushed. What'd you do to that guy in the diner, anyway?"

"Just grabbed his hand real hard."

"He was in pain."

"That's the whole idea."

"Lenny's bigger than you, and you laid him out pretty fast. What're you, six feet?"

"He's big, but slow. I'm five-eleven, actually."

She got on top of me but lay flat this time and kissed me. "Wanna fuck again?"

"Give me a little time, okay?" I said.

"Okay, I'll give you a little time. But I'm ready now."

She kissed me hard and sucked my tongue into her mouth. She closed her lips on my tongue and sucked it as if it were my penis. Then we both started laughing.

"That's a tongue job," she said.

A few minutes later, after we'd spent some time tickling each other and laughing, I rolled her over and scooted down until my head was between her legs. I kissed and nibbled at her strong thighs, rubbed my face against their silky skin. I licked her bare pubis, moved my head back and forth as I slowly ran my tongue up and down between her wet lips.

"Oh, yeah, do that some more," she said, her voice low and smoky. "Do that a *lot* more."

She talked on as I licked and sucked her, and sometimes she laughed. After a while, she gasped for breath and squeezed my shoulders with her hands. She pounded her head back into the pillow again and again and squeezed my head between her thighs.

Another pair of headlights passed over the windows and I lifted my head a moment to catch her in the light, her lush body stretched out before me, pale and soft.

"Don't stop!" she cried.

I lowered my head and continued.

After much writhing and moaning, she slowed down gradually and made purring sounds as she ran her fingers through my hair. She pulled me up to her, kissed me.

"I don't know about you," she said, "but I gotta have a cigarette."

Chapter 3

I dreamed of my last job. A rich woman in her sixties, apparently very healthy and vital. Sonny boy never liked her, and he was sick of waiting for his inheritance, simple as that. Once he found me—which is very hard, by the way; the only people who find me are the ones who are very serious about their business—he found out I don't come cheap, so he had to scrape together enough money to pay me. He sounded shaky and nervous over the phone, and I figured he was either a drug addict or a gambler and he needed money to feed something that had its claws sunk into his back, and he wanted Mommy's money. He said he saw my price as a good investment. I never met him in person, of course. I never do. It was all done over prepaid cell phones, and always is. He sent the money to a mail drop I have in San Bernardino. I have several all over the country and even a few in other countries. I told him to make sure a lot of people saw him on the night of the job.

I went around to the back of the house and broke the window in the back door. I wanted it to look like a break-in. Upstairs in her bedroom, I put a pillow over her face while she was sleeping and smothered her to death. Then I tore the place up a little, stole some jewels to make it look like a robbery.

That's what I dreamed about, what I always dreamed about—the last job. The act of doing it. She fought, but she wasn't very strong. When I was done, I lifted the pillow. I was close enough to see her in the dark, and she looked like a grandmother, a plump, silver-haired woman with no teeth in her head. That's what I dreamed about, too. Her face. I always dreamed about the faces, and there had been a lot of them over the years. It wasn't that I felt guilty, because I didn't. But those faces haunted my dreams, anyway.

I was retiring because I didn't want to dream about anymore faces. The ones already lodged in my head were enough. I had more money than I'd ever need. I was through with it, and it felt good.

But not when I was dreaming. I was always on the job in my dreams, and I always loved it.

I awoke with a gasp, sat up in bed in the dark.

I was in bed alone. The digital clock radio on Carmen's nightstand read 4:12. I reached under the pillow. My 9mm Browning Hi-Power was there where I'd put it before going to sleep the night before, safety on. Carmen had been in the bathroom and had not seen it. I did not carry the gun on me unless I was working, and sometimes not even then, but kept it in the suitcase, and I liked to keep it close when I slept in a strange place.

The doorknob jiggled and I heard a key inserted into the lock.

I grabbed the gun with my right hand, turned off the safety, rolled off the bed, and hunkered down on one knee, the gun aimed at the door, my right hand cupped in my left.

Carmen pushed the door open and came in. She didn't see me on the floor beside the bed.

"Where were you?" I said as I stood.

She cried out as she spun around with a jerk. "Jeez, you scared the hell outta me."

I turned on the bedside lamp. "Didn't mean to startle you," I said. She wore her red bellyshirt and denim cut-offs.

"I went for a walk," she said. "I couldn't sleep." She pointed wide-eyed at the gun. "What's *that* for?"

I flipped the safety catch again. "For protection."

Carmen kicked off her shoes, dropped her cut-offs, and snatched her purse off the table as she headed for the bathroom. "I fell down in the mud. I'm gonna take a quick shower."

"Okay," I said. "Are you all right?"

"Oh, yeah, I'm fine. Just got my hands and arms dirty."

I looked at her hands. There was something on them, something dark—a deep red.

In the bathroom, she closed the door. The shower hissed to life.

I stood there, naked and frowning, as I stared at the bathroom door. Something odd had just happened, but I hadn't isolated it yet. I was already disturbed by the fact that she had not awakened me when she left. I was typically a very light sleeper. I must have been more tired than I thought. Or she knew how to be very stealthy.

I looked at the round table by the front windows. Something was missing.

What was it?

My wallet was on my nightstand. I put my gun back under the pillow.

My eyes returned to the round table, to the spot where Carmen's purse had stood a moment ago.

The key. That was it. Where was the room key? It was not on the table. I looked over at the writing desk, which came complete with motel stationary, but it wasn't there, either. I frowned at the bathroom door.

Had Carmen taken the key into the shower with her? Why? *To wash it off?* I thought.

I fell down in the mud, she'd said.

And what was on her hands besides mud?

I turned my ear to the window and listened. It sounded like it was still raining outside, if only a sprinkle.

Why go for a walk in the rain? At night? In a strange place?

I flipped on the overhead light. I looked down at the cut-offs on the floor, picked them up. There was a wet spot along the tattered bottom on one side. I recognized it immediately as blood.

She opened the bathroom door and startled me. She came into the room naked with her purse in one hand, the room key in the other, and put them on the table.

"What're you doin'?" she said. She looked at her shorts in my hand, then at me again.

"Where did this blood come from?" I said.

She pointed down, and I saw the cut on her left knee. It was still bleeding. "I told you, I fell down. Do you have a first-aid kit in your car?"

"Yes, I do." I put on my boxers and a T-shirt from my suitcase, grabbed my keys, and went out into the drizzly night to the car. The kit was in the trunk. I got it and went back inside. "What in the world were you doing, going for a walk in the rain in the middle of the night?"

"That's one of my favorite things," she said.

"Oh. Okay, if you say so. Just don't sing it. Why did you take the room key into the bathroom with you?"

"It had mud all over it. I washed it off. Why so many questions?"

I shrugged. "Here, let's get a bandage on that cut."

She sat on the edge of the bed and I knelt in front of her. I cleaned the cut carefully. It looked like it had been delivered with a knife, a quick slice with a blade.

In my line of work, you become acquainted with wounds and their origins. The cut did not look like it had been sustained in a fall. It was much too smooth and straight, as if someone had simply swiped a blade over the skin just above the knee.

I looked up at her and thought, *What are you up to?*

I sprayed disinfectant on the cut, and wrapped it in a long strip of gauze.

"What about *you*?" she said.

"What about me?"

"I could ask *you* a few questions. Like what're you doin' with a gun? What computer analyst carries a gun?"

"Like I said, the gun's for protection."

She nodded with a disbelieving smile. "Yeah. Who are you, *really*?"

I taped the bandage with the white tape provided in the kit. "There you go," I said.

"Thanks," she said.

"Sure," I said as I stood. "It's pretty superficial, it doesn't need stitches." She was naked, and I could not prevent my eyes from moving slowly down her body, then back up again. It was a thing of beauty, her body, and it drew my eyes to it like metal shavings being drawn to a magnet.

"Sorry for snapping at you," she said. She stood and put her arms around me, kissed me. "You don't mind a little bandage, do you?"

"As long as you're not in any pain." I squeezed each side of her ass in my hands.

She nipped my lower lip between her teeth, almost hard enough to hurt. "A little pain never hurt anybody," she whispered. A little laugh. "Listen to me. I'm a bad girl."

I lifted my right hand and slapped one cheek with a sharp sound. "You need a spanking?" I said.

Carmen giggled as she reached into my boxers through the fly. She wrapped her hand around my cock and pulled it out, stroked it. As she knelt in front of me, she pulled down my boxers. I stepped out of them, sat down on the bed. She took me into her mouth, took my balls in her hand. She made loud slurping sounds as I became immersed in what she was doing to me.

She stood and pushed me onto my back on the bed. She climbed onto me.

"Do it to me," she whispered, her trembling hands pressed to my chest. "Fuck me. Now, right now."

I pushed her off of me and rolled over on top of her, between her legs. I reached over to the nightstand and grabbed a condom. I tore the wrapper open with my teeth, tossed it to the floor and quickly put the rubber on. I entered her hard. She trembled all over as she clutched at me with her fingers, as she dug her heels into my ass. I pounded into her hard and fast, and she kept up with me, moving with each thrust of my hips. She squirmed and flailed beneath me, almost as if she were trying to fight me off. But she wasn't. We struggled with each other — that's what it felt like for a while, struggling — and the bed thumped the wall every time I plunged into her. Someone in the next room pounded on the wall behind the bed, but we ignored it.

"Fuck me harder," she growled. "*Harder*, goddammit."

I slammed into her, and each time, her teeth clacked together in her open mouth.

When she came, she cried out several times and went wild underneath me. She nearly knocked me off the bed. I came with her.

I rolled off her and we lay there across the bed, sweaty, staring at the ceiling, catching our breaths.

She found my hand with hers and squeezed it.

I couldn't remember ever having sex so…so *hard*. I had never been with anyone like Carmen before.

"I need a cigarette," she said as she slowly got up and went to her purse on the table. "Want one?"

I said yes, and she came back with two cigarettes in her mouth and a lighter in hand. She lit them both and handed one to me, got the ashtray from the nightstand and set it on the bed between us. She lay on her right side, propped up on an elbow, facing me.

"What's a computer programmer, or analyst, or consultant, or whatever the hell, doing with a gun?" she said.

"I travel a lot. I keep it for protection."

"Who did you think was coming in here earlier?"

"I didn't know, I'd just woke up."

"Mm. You shoulda known it was gonna be me."

"Yeah. I should've."

After we finished our cigarettes, we got back into bed, with only a sheet pulled over us.

Carmen nestled in the crook of my arm, stroked her hand up and down my chest and belly. "I like you, Benedetti," she said, her voice throaty.

"I like you, too, Mattox." I lay my head back and closed my eyes. She continued to run her fingertips up and down my front.

"We just gonna part ways tomorrow in Sacramento?" Carmen said.

I shrugged. "I don't know. You got relatives in Los Angeles?"

"Yeah, y'know, I gotta cousin lives in Placentia, some town down there. I guess I could go pay her a visit. Pretty disgusting name, huh? Placentia?"

"Was your sister expecting you?"

"No. My sister and me, see, we don't get along so well. I'd probably be better off at my cousin's."

"You get along well with your cousin?"

"I hardly know her. That's a plus in this case."

I said, "You need money? Is that why you're looking for family?"

"Not really. I got some money, but it ain't gonna last much longer. What I really need is a place to stay while I look for a job and then find a place to live, that kinda thing."

A warning alarm went off silently in my head. I was not looking for a woman to live with. I wanted to do some traveling, and I already had my heart set on doing it alone, blissfully alone to do as I pleased when I pleased. I planned to catch up on my reading while I lounged on a variety of beaches and beside a series of hotel swimming pools.

On the other hand, I found that I felt rather attached to Carmen Mattox. She was, for one thing, the best sex I'd ever had, hands down. She was beautiful. She sounded uneducated, but she was clearly no dummy.

If she wanted to go down to Los Angeles with me and stay with her cousin, that would be fine. But I firmly told myself she was *not* moving in with me. I had to be extra firm with myself, though, as I looked down at her in bed beside me, her head nestled in a shimmering pool of red hair that spilled over my arm and her pillow.

Her lashes looked longer when her eyes were closed. Her hair framed an oval face with strong features and deep-set eyes. I looked at the tiny, almost invisible dimple in her left cheek. It deepened when she smiled, and the left side of her mouth turned up more than the right. But now she slept.

I rolled over onto my right side and hoped to do the same.

I eventually drifted off, and as I swam through sleep, I saw those faces. So many faces.

Chapter 4

I guess I'd started that vacation a little early. I'd started it in my head, because I wasn't thinking clearly, wasn't seeing things straight. My brain was on vacation. I figured I'd done my last job, I was home free. Out of the life for good. And I let my guard down. Under normal circumstances, Carmen would have set off more than one silent alarm inside me. Why did she lie about her knee? Who did it to her? Where had she gone in the middle of the night? Had she cut her knee herself, for some reason? But while I asked all those questions of myself when she first showed me the cut, they didn't linger in search of answers.

My first thought the next morning was of having sex with Carmen. My second thought was that I'd probably want to have sex with Carmen again. Right away.

I rolled over, but she wasn't there. I heard sounds in the bathroom. The shower was running with a whispery hiss. The clock radio on her nightstand read 10:02.

I usually woke up at six every morning, whether I had an alarm set or not. But I'd slept through it that day.

I sat up on the edge of the bed and lit a cigarette.

I got up and went to the sink, washed my hands, cigarette between my lips. The ash dropped off the end and landed in the sink. I turned on the clock radio on Carmen's side of the bed. Caught the tail-end of an Eagles song.

I went back to the nightstand and put my cigarette on the edge of the ashtray, sat down again and yawned, scrubbed my face with both hands. It was later than I'd intended to get up. The temperature probably was already pushing a hundred degrees out there. I'd wanted to get started early, before the sun had its claws in the earth. As I took a drag on my cigarette, something on the radio caught my attention.

"—carnival owner, Leonard Dupree, known as Lenny to his family and friends," a woman's voice said.

I thought of the carnival where I'd met Carmen—Dupree Amusements, Inc.

"Dupree was brutally stabbed thirty-two times," the newscaster continued, "and almost decapitated. The carnival-owner was found in his trailer on the carnival grounds. The Dupree Entertainments Carnival had been in Garver for two days and nights and had been scheduled to move on today, but Dupree's murder has altered their plans. The Garver Police Department and the Shasta County Sheriff's Office are working together on the investigation. They have released no further information to the press, although a press conference is expected later today. A source close to the investigation, who wishes to remain anonymous, claims there's evidence to support the theory that this is the work of the Sundown Killer, a serial killer who terrorized Tehama and Shasta Counties back in 2002 and 2003. The Sundown Killer was never apprehended, but the killings stopped in late 2003."

The newscaster went on to say that Dupree's killing was somehow similar to the Sundown Killer's victims, although no further details were available.

I sat on the bed and smoked my cigarette and thought about that a while as the shower ran in the bathroom.

I remembered what Carmen had said to Lenny as I was approaching them at the back of the tent: *What did I tell you, huh? Didn't I say if you ever touch me again, I'll kill you? Huh? Didn't I?*

But I was with her from then on. When would she have had time to kill Lenny?

Oh, shit, Carmen had said at the carnival gate, *I left my purse in the trailer*

How long had I waited after that? Had it been five minutes? Ten? Fifteen? I couldn't remember how long it was, exactly, only that it seemed to take longer than it should have, and that I was a little annoyed by the time she got back. But I'd kept it to myself.

Had she gone back to kill Lenny? If so, she had done it with plenty of speed. Eight or ten minutes were annoying while waiting around, but to *kill* someone—that would take a while longer, especially if you included the walk through the carnival there and back. If she'd managed to do that herself—and cover her tracks as well as she had—well, then, I had picked up the wrong beautiful woman.

On the other hand, if I accused her of murder and it turned out I wasn't thinking clearly, it would most likely piss her off.

And what was that business about a serial killer?

Whenever I went to a carnival when I was a kid, my mom would give me some money and this warning: "Stay away from the carnies, you hear me?" She never gave me a clear explanation for that warning, but she repeated it every time I went.

I suddenly wondered what the hell I was doing on the road with, of all things, a carny. Because that was what she was, no two ways about it. She was one of the people my mother warned me about without ever explaining why. If my mom knew, she'd probably slap me. But there was a lot about me my dear old mother knew nothing about. A lot of things she'd slap me for, too.

Then the bathroom door opened and the news cut for a commercial.

Carmen came out naked, drying her hair, and the sight of her naked body reminded me instantly of why I was on the road with her. The gauze bandage on her leg was gone and had been replaced by a couple of Band-Aids from the first aid kit. She tossed the towel on the bed as she came around to my side. She stood in front of me, bent down and kissed the top of my head, and said, "Whatta you wanna do to me?"

I stood and took her in my arms. "You name it," I said.

"No, you *name* it." She whispered in my ear, "Whatta you wanna do to me? Anything you want."

I got hard against her.

She pushed down on my shoulders and I sat down on the bed again. She knelt in front of me.

"Anything," she said as she took me into her mouth.

As she worked on me, I spoke with a tremble in my voice. "Well, I'm…pretty easy…to please. I'm a…a meat and potatoes kinda guy. Nothing you could do…could be any sweeter than what you're doing…right now."

She brought me to the edge with her mouth, then stopped. She ripped a condom-wrapper open with her teeth and removed the rubber.

"C'mon, sit back against the headboard," she said.

I got on the bed and sat up against the pillows and the cheap, wobbly headboard. She came up and straddled me, stood over me for a moment. It was a beautiful view, looking up at her shaved pussy and the bottom scoops of her wonderful breasts. Then she slid the condom over my erection, got down on her knees, and guided me into her slowly.

"Now," she whispered, "don't move."

She put her arms around my neck and kissed me, and I put mine around her. We sat like that for a long time, just kissing while I was inside her. Once in a while, she would squeeze me with her vaginal muscles, and when she did that, I always took in a sharp breath.

After a long time, she moved her hips, slid up my erection, stopped for a moment, then slowly slid down again.

She sat up straight, tipped her head back, and closed her eyes. I watched her. She reached down and fingered her clitoris as she moved on me.

I wondered if she could have killed Lenny.

I heard my mother say, She is, after all, Steven, a carny.

But those thoughts were in the back shadows of my mind. All I could focus on was Carmen, and what it felt like being inside her.

She gradually moved faster and faster until she pounded down on me. She flexed those muscles in there, and I exploded while she pressed her open mouth over mine.

She kept pounding me and I was glad my erection held until she cried out and shuddered and bucked in my arms.

Carmen fell forward on me, pushing me back against the pillows. She kissed my shoulder and I kissed her neck. I was still inside her.

She whispered in my ear, "Wait'll you see what I do to you on the road."

I laughed. It startled me because it was a real laugh that I felt inside before releasing it. I hadn't experienced one of those in a while. I pulled her upright in front of me and kissed her deeply. It was a sudden impulse. It felt good.

"I've changed my mind," she said as she got up.

"About what?"

She stood up on the bed, then hopped to the floor. She turned to me and smiled. "I'm goin' to Los Angeles, see my cousin. As long as I can see you, too."

I returned her smile. "Sounds good to me."

"C'mon, let's get outta here," she said with a clap of her hands. "Check-out time's in fifteen minutes."

I put on a green pullover shirt with three buttons at the neck, charcoal slacks. Carmen wore the same cut-offs with a red T-shirt that read "Genius At Work." We put our bags in the trunk and got in the car.

It was a grey, overcast day. Once again it was hot and the humidity was thick. The rain had stopped, but the dark clouds had not gone away.

As I drove out of the parking lot, I stopped at the exit because there were three police cars parked near the entrance to the truck stop across the street.

"Wonder what happened over there?" Carmen said as I drove away and got back on the freeway.

Chapter 5

We stopped at a Denny's a couple of exits south of Pantyhose Junction and had breakfast.

While we ate in a booth, Carmen put her bare foot between my thighs and fondled me with her toes. "You never answered my question," she whispered across the table.

"What question?"

"What do you want to do to me?"

"Like I said, I'm a meat-and-potatoes guy. And right now, thanks to you, I'm the most satisfied and fulfilled meat-and-potatoes guy on the face of the earth."

"Oh, come on, you must have some deep, dark fantasy. Something you've never told anyone?"

I'd had the same conversation before with another girlfriend. She wanted me to tell her about my secret fantasy, the sexual fantasy I'd never shared with anyone, so she could fulfill it. She refused to believe that I had no secret fantasy. It bothered her so much, that she ended up convincing herself that I *did* have a secret fantasy, but it was so depraved and upsetting that I was afraid to share it with her, and that was one of the main reasons she'd left me.

Carmen continued to prod at me with her toes.

I said, "Why is it so difficult to believe that I harbor no secret fantasies? Look, I *love* sex, okay? I love sex with *you*. What we did is what I like to do." I leaned forward, lowered my voice, and said with a smirk, "And if you don't stop that, I'm going to have an erection walking out of here and we're *both* going to be embarrassed."

She chuckled. "Speak for yourself, honey."

We got back on the road, and I turned on the radio and looked for some local news. I wanted to see if any mention was made of Lenny's murder, and there was a chance a local news station would know what was going on at the Pantyhose Junction truck stop, where those three cruisers had been parked. It was almost noon, and the network newscasts would be coming on any minute, followed by a local report. I found the network news and left it there.

"Can we put on some music?" Carmen said.

"After the news."

She put one bare foot up on the seat and rested her chin on her knee. "Is it a long trip? To Los Angeles?"

"It's long, but it feels a lot longer."

The local news came on and I focused my attention on it. "A trucker was brutally murdered in his cab sometime in the early hours of this morning. Earle Lee Baker, fifty-eight, of Spokane, Washington, was found in his truck behind the local Pantyhose Junction, where he had been stabbed multiple times. Police have released no other details of the murder, but speculation has already begun about the possibility that this is the work of the Sundown Killer."

"There it is again," I said. "The Sundown Killer."

I used to be a news junkie. I had CNN on all the time, only listened to news-talk radio stations, read half a dozen papers a day, and even more online. Then I realized how tensed up I was one evening while I sat watching CNN. I came to realize I was tense all the time, and I started to wonder if my daily diet of death, disaster, and catastrophe could have something to do with it. I stopped cold turkey. I spent more time outside, went for long walks, and even lost some weight. I became a calmer person. After some time had passed, I eased back into it. I started taking a look at CNN now and then, just briefly. Or I'd read the business section, maybe the sports section. I even bought *USA Today* a couple of times, America's favorite colorful picturebook, and absorbed the news in charts, graphs, and photos.

Back then, I probably would have known every detail of the Sundown Killer story there was to know. But by 2003, I was just beginning to hesitantly return to the news, and it wasn't a big nationwide story, so I knew nothing about it.

What had Carmen done when she'd gone out last night? She'd taken her purse with her. Maybe it held a weapon. I would have to check first chance I got.

Why a trucker? Why that particular trucker? I thought back over our meal at Pantyhose Junction.

I remembered walking back into the diner after going to the restroom and finding that man tugging on Carmen's arm, trying to get her to go with him to his truck.

Get your filthy hands off me or I'll kill you! Carmen had said.

I looked at her. I kept glancing at the road—the traffic was thin, and it was a straight shot ahead—but I really *looked* at her. It was a look I'd given to a lot of people just before they died, and it made them freak out, because they—every last one of them—*recognized* that look. They knew it meant I was going to kill them. When I gave people that look, they got worried. Some cried. Others wet themselves. I gave Carmen that look because I wanted her to worry. By the time I asked the first question about what she'd been up to last night, I wanted her to be nervous, on edge.

Carmen laughed and said, "*What* in the *hell* is your *problem?*" When I didn't respond, she said, "Well? You got somethin' to say, *say* it."

I stopped looking at her and faced front. She was right. What the hell was I doing, making faces at her. It was then, at that very moment, that I realized I was in a relationship.

When you're just a couple of people having fun, life is easy and honest, and there's no need to make faces. But as soon as you step into that big block of gooey emotional concrete called A Relationship, which immediately hardens around your feet, then the face-making and the game-playing begins. At least, that's the way I tend to see it.

Relationships had always sneaked up on me, my whole life. They'd never come up the front walk and rung the doorbell; instead, they stealthily entered through the back door while I wasn't paying attention. My first girlfriend, Ginger Crane, didn't come along until my freshman year in college—I was a late starter—and I'd known her since we were high school freshmen. She'd just broken up with her boyfriend and I spent some time with her to cheer her up, and before you knew it, *bam*, there we were in bed, and it had gone straight from being a wonderful night to being a relationship. It was a great relationship, though, until my friend Mark told me the truth that everyone else could see but me—she was with me only to piss off her ex-boyfriend, Archie Flagg, a friend of mine, an athlete whom I often helped with his homework. I hadn't given much thought to Flagg, mostly because he already had a new girlfriend and didn't seem to be mourning his relationship with Ginger. The fact that our relationship did not bother Flagg made Ginger furious.

For a few days, there, we had sex that was so good, we could almost forget we were in a car. She was *amazing* when she got angry about something. Then, one evening, we went out to dinner and she said she had something to tell me. I told her I wanted to go first. I told her I knew what she was up to, and I wasn't going to stand there and let her make me look like a buffoon, so I told her we were through. She smiled and said, "What a coincidence! I wanted to meet with you here tonight because I wanted to break up with you."

Relationships can sneak up on you, all right. They can do that coming in, and they can do it going out.

I looked at Carmen and smiled.

"Who's this Sundown Killer?" I said.

Carmen looked straight ahead as she curled her feet up under her on the seat. She frowned, but not at me. "I don't know."

"You don't know anything about the Sundown Killer?"

She shrugged and her frown deepened. "Some serial killer, I guess, I dunno."

A lot of time passed while I thought.

"I heard about Lenny on the radio this morning," I said. I looked at her. "Heard all about it."

Her eyebrows slowly rose as she turned to me. "Heard all about what?"

"What happened to him."

"Well…what…what happened to him?"

I saw nothing in her face, no dead giveaways. She looked genuinely curious.

"He was killed."

Her eyes widened. "Lenny was killed?"

I nodded. "Stabbed to death. They seem to think it might be the Sundown Killer striking again."

She made a *hmph* sound. "It coulda been anybody. Lenny pissed off everyone he ever met."

"How did you manage to get involved with that guy?" I asked.

Carmen sighed. "He took care of me when I needed it. It was Lenny's carnival I ran off with, back when he was travelin' that part of the country. There was this boy named Robby who worked for him, and all I wanted was to be with him. I did odd jobs around the carnival, worked some of the games. Then I found out Robby was already fucking two of the girls in the carnival. *And* he was a heroin addict. But by then, I was a good distance from home. Lenny cheered me up, gave me work, kept me going."

"Is that when you got involved with him?"

She nodded. "The first time. Like I said, I been in and out of the carnival over the years. But it was always Lenny's carnival, nobody else's. Lenny was kind of a good guy back then. He's gotten mean over the years, mean and angry. Personally, I think he's got a brain tumor, or somethin', that's how drastic the change has been. Drastic, but it's been slow. He pisses me off, but he's really kinda...sad, y'know?"

"You said he hit you."

She said nothing for a while, then, "Yeah. He hit me." Without looking at me, she said, "Can we put on some music now?"

I found some music and we said nothing more for a long time. Carmen put her head back and closed her eyes. She slept for about forty-five minutes. Then she lifted her head, looked over at me, and smiled. She stretched, rubbed her eyes, ran her fingers through her hair and released a long, luxurious sigh. The she looked at me for a while with a gentle smile on her lips.

"Are you some kind of cop?" she said.

"No, I'm no kind of cop."

"So, you don't work for, like, the FBI or the CIA?"

"I told you, I'm retired."

"Whatever. Then you haven't worked for the—"

"No. I've always been self-employed." I looked over and could tell she was about to ask another question. "Look, is this entirely necessary? I've already told you where I've lived, what I used to do. What more can I do? If you'd like, I suppose I can make up an alternate story and tell it to you. Would you like that?"

"Mm," she said as she shrugged. "You just don't seem like a computer salesman."

"Consultant. A computer consultant."

"Whatever. You just don't seem like one, is all."

I smiled. "What's your idea of how a computer consultant should look?"

"Oh, I don't know. Glasses, maybe. Bad haircuts. Pocket protectors. Pants a little high over white socks. Like that."

"Well, I hope I've changed your mind about computer consultants." I smiled.

"Oh, you're no consultant, I'm convinced of that."

I laughed and shook my head. "Okay, if you say so."

Carmen leaned over the center console and nibbled on my ear. I laughed and shook my head. "That tickles," I said. When she unzipped my pants, I said, "Whoa, what are you doing?"

"Ever get a handjob while you're drivin'?" she said with a girlish laugh. She reached into my pants, into my boxers, and pulled out my cock.

"I don't know if this is a good idea," I said.

"You think *this* is unsafe, you oughtta see what happens when I try to give you a blowjob at the wheel." She stroked me as she spoke, leaning close. "This doesn't get in your way, and it feels sooo nice, doesn't it?"

I put my hand on her wrist and pushed her away from me.

"What's wrong?" she said.

"I can't do this," I said. "It'll get all over my pants."

She laughed. "Don't worry about your pants, sweety. I'll wash them for you when we get to your place."

Carmen continued to stroke my erection. I worked hard to focus on the road. There was a slow-moving eighteen-wheeler in front of me, so I went around him on the left. As I drove by, a thunderous honk came from the truck. I turned to my right, but all I could see was the truck's door. I realized he could see into my cab, and that was why he'd honked. I smiled as I honked back.

"There's, uh…some Kleenex in the glovebox," I said. "We're gonna need them."

She opened the glovebox with her free hand and took out the small packet of tissues, pulled out a couple.

"Oh, god," I said as I pushed my hips up once, hard.

I ejaculated all over the bottom of the steering wheel, but Carmen kept me from getting any on my pants. She laughed as she took more tissues from the packet and cleaned off the wheel.

When she was done, she rolled down the window and tossed the wadded tissues out of the car.

Carmen leaned over the center console and put her hand on the back of my head, closed it over a fistful of hair, and pulled my head back slightly.

"Let's stop at the next cut-off so you can fuck me," she said, then she licked my cheek.

I laughed and said, "I can't tell you how much I love your enthusiasm, Mattox. It's…refreshing. And very tempting."

"So pull over."

"Look, for reasons of my own, I'd rather not do anything that might get the attention of a highway patrolman, okay?

Pulling over to have sex in the car would probably be the kind of thing that would get his attention."

She flopped back in her seat.

"I wish you'd put your seatbelt on," I said. Mine was in place.

"You and your—you know, Benedetti, you're too uptight." She fastened the belt around her. "You need to live on the edge once in a while. Keeps you young."

"On the edge, huh?"

"Sure. Drive around with your seatbelt off for a while. Walk against the light. Run with the scissors. Little victories like that, they're what keep life interesting."

I smiled. "You like getting away with things, don't you?"

Half her mouth turned up. "Anything I can."

"Ever get away with murder?" I asked.

She flinched and her half-smile disappeared, her face relaxed, then she frowned as her entire body stiffened with tension. "Wha…what did you say?"

"I was just kidding around. I asked if you'd ever gotten away with murder, that's all."

"Why would you ask something like that?" she whispered as she turned away from me and looked out the window to her right.

"I'm sorry if I offended you, Carmen," I said. "It was just a joke. I didn't mean anything by it."

Her reaction was interesting. The question had disturbed her.

She did not respond for a while, just stared out the window.

"I accept your apology," she finally said. "But I'm still horny." She turned and gave me a smile that looked a little sad.

Carmen unfastened her seatbelt, slid down in the seat, lifted her ass up, and removed her cut-offs. She let them drop to the floorboard.

"What are you doing?" I said, a little surprised.

She pushed the seatback down and lay flat in the seat. "What I *always* do when I'm really horny but my man is unavailable." She put her heels up on the seat's edge, her knees up, and reached down between her thighs with her right hand. She smiled up at me and said, "You wanna see how fast I can get myself off?"

I laughed another of those genuine laughs and said, "Okay."

She put her bare feet up on the dashboard and bit on her lower lip as her hand moved furiously between her legs. It moved so fast, it was a blur. In about thirty seconds, she thrust her hips up a few times, cried out and even laughed.

Carmen grinned up at me and said, "You should see the look on your face."

I could only imagine. Watching her masturbate made me hungry for her. I reached over and stroked her smooth thigh. She grabbed my hand and put it between her legs, where it was wet and hot. I stroked her for a while, slid my finger inside her.

An SUV honked at me as I swerved into the left line right in front of him. I couldn't do it—it was too distracting, and I was unable to drive safely. So I pulled my hand away.

She continued to stroke herself, but not as intensely as before. She raised the seatback again and sat there smiling at me, naked from the waist down.

"That was fun," she said. "See? Not *all* women have trouble having orgasms. I'm *very* orgasmic."

"From now on, I'm calling you Speedy."

She laughed, and I realized how much I loved that sound, how much I enjoyed bringing it out in her.

Just sex, I thought. *It was going to be just sex with a beautiful woman, for one night. Now I'm sitting here thinking about how much I love her laugh. Where did I go wrong?*

My mistake had been having sex with her in the first place. Some people had addictive personalities, and some people—far fewer, of course—were addictive. Sex with Carmen was addictive. Carmen herself was somehow addictive. As I drove beneath the thin clouds along Interstate 5, I had to wrestle fiercely with the urge to pull over at the next possible spot, put our seats down and get on top of her. I reached over and stroked Carmen's thigh again. I was having withdrawals and needed, at least, to touch her.

"We could always stop at another motel," Carmen said.

"That's a pretty juicy temptation, Carmen," I said. "But let's see how far we can get before the urge to pull over and get a room becomes too great."

I noticed my foot was a bit heavy on the pedal. I eased back a little and kept at the speed limit. But for some reason, I felt rushed by an urgent need to go home to my house in Laurel Canyon, home where I had, at the very least, the cozy illusion of safety and security. It was as if we were being pursued by something deeply and profoundly dark. Not a person, but a…a *shape*, a constantly moving, undulating mass of darkness hurtling toward us like a flying patch of midnight. I shook my head sharply and rubbed my eyes with thumb and finger, trying to eject the thought. It had come out of nowhere and had altered my mood entirely.

Chapter 6

While Carmen dozed, I searched the radio dial until I found an all-news station. I listened to farm reports and weather updates—more summer rain was on the way—and finally:

"Police in Garver have released a surveillance-camera photo of the woman they believe to have killed carnival-owner Leonard Dupree. Authorities still won't say whether or not they believe this woman to be the Sundown Killer, a serial killer who stalked the highways in Tehama and Shasta Counties a decade ago."

A photo. I had to see it. Where could I find a television?

In another motel room.

Local newscasts usually ran at five or six in the evening. I decided to keep driving until then.

I watched Carmen sleep.

What was I doing? I wasn't sure. All I knew was how good she made me feel. I'd been single for a long time, about ten years. I saw the occasional prostitute during that time, but didn't go on a single date. Then, out of the blue, this quirky, funny woman who was also stunningly gorgeous walked into my life, and I had the best sex I'd ever had in my life.

The voice of reason spoke up in the back of my head: *But what if she's a killer?*

The voice of my libido replied, *Nobody's perfect.*

———

I drove for hours through the barren landscape spotted occasionally with barns, speckled with grazing cows.

Carmen wanted to drive for a while, so I let her.

"Nice car," she said. "It's been a while since I've driven anything."

"You *do* have a license, don't you?"

"Yeah, but it's expired."

"Pull over," I said.

"What?"

"Take the next exit and pull into that gas station."

"But I just got on the freeway, why do I have to—"

"Just do it."

"All right." She turned off Interstate 5 and pulled into a 76 gas station.

As soon as she stopped the car, I reached over, turned off the engine and took the key from the ignition. "I'm driving," I said.

"But that wasn't very long," she said plaintively.

I got out and went around the car to the driver's side. Carmen climbed over the center console and got in the passenger seat.

"If we get pulled over, or something," I said, "your expired license will only make trouble for us."

She watched me as I got back on the freeway. A smile grew slowly on her face.

"You're afraid of the cops," she said.

"Why do you say that?"

"Because you're so worried about them."

"I'm worried about them seeing *you*," I said. "I heard about you on the radio earlier, Carmen, while you were sleeping. Has it ever occurred to you that you might be a *suspect* in Lenny's murder?"

"Why me?"

"I don't know. Maybe because he wouldn't leave you alone?"

"I left because he wouldn't leave me alone."

"But you had to go back and kill him before you left, didn't you?"

She turned to me, lips parted, and just stared at me for a moment. Then: "You really believe that?"

"I don't know yet," I said as I took the next exit off the freeway. "But we'll find out soon." I pulled off the freeway and into a Motel 6 and stopped under the portico in front of the office. "Be right back," I said. I went in, paid for the room, and took the key back out to the car. I pulled into the courtyard-like parking lot in front of the U-shaped building. I carried our bags up the outdoor stairs to the second level and unlocked our room.

Inside, Carmen smiled and said, "Okay, let me get this straight. You think I might be a killer, but you still wanna fuck me."

I fished my condoms out of my suitcase and put the box on the nightstand. Then I took her in my arms and held her close. Our lips were almost touching when I said, "Yeah. That's right. Guess that makes me the crazy one, huh?" I kissed her hard and our tongues moved together. I reached under her T-shirt and squeezed a breast with one hand while I put the other on her ass and pulled her close against my erection.

She pulled back and took the T-shirt off over her head, dropped the cut-offs, kicked off her sneakers. Then she pulled my shirt over my head and fumbled with my belt until it was unbuckled. I took off my shoes and stepped out of my pants as she took them off me. I hung up my clothes, then took off my boxers as she pulled back the covers on the bed.

I pushed the Power button on the remote control bolted to the nightstand on my side and the television came on. According to my watch, it was twelve minutes to five.

I got on the bed and stacked the pillows up against the wall, sat up against them. I smiled at her and said, "Why don't you come sit on my lap, little girl. Tell Santa what you want for Christmas."

She laughed as she put the condom on me, then straddled me and lowered herself onto my erection. She just sat there and we kissed for a while. She started moving on me in slow circular motions.

"Why are you afraid of the cops?" she whispered.

I said nothing.

"Are they after you for something?" She ran her fingers down my chest and belly slowly, then lifted her hands and did it again. "What did you do?"

I smiled and closed my eyes, leaned my head back and enjoyed the sensation of being inside her, of her fingers on my chest and belly.

"Did you kill someone?" she whispered. "Is that what I see in your eyes?"

I opened my eyes and she looked into them.

"Is that murder I'm seeing in there, that looks so serious?" She smiled.

After a long time, I whispered, "I'll tell you if you'll tell me."

"Tell you what?"

"Did you kill Lenny? Did you go back there and stab him to death, then come back out to my car with your purse like nothing in the world was wrong? Huh? Did you do that?"

She put a hand to each side of my face and kissed me. We stayed that way for a while.

Over her shoulder I checked my watch. It was a couple of minutes before five. I looked at the TV. A cartoon was on. I reached over and flipped through the stations until I found one showing a commercial for a local auto sales place and left it there.

"What are you doing?" she said as she stopped moving on me.

"I want to catch the local news. They have a picture of the killer. I want to see if it's you."

I watched her for a reaction, but there was nothing

"A picture, huh?" she said as she fondled my nipple.

"From a surveillance camera."

The Five O' Clock News Team came on with much fanfare and overproduction. Carmen kept her back to the television.

"Aren't you interested at all?" I said. "Even a little?"

She squeezed me with her vaginal muscles and I closed my eyes a moment and moaned. "I'm interested in you," she whispered. "Why are the cops after you? What have you done?" She moved her hips again in slow circles.

"Like I said, I'll tell you if you'll tell me."

"What if there's nothing to tell?"

It was the top story.

"Do you know this woman?" the anchorman said.

The picture was blurry, but it was, without a doubt, Carmen. I recognized my shoulder right beside her, but fortunately, my face was not included in the photo. It had been taken somewhere in the carnival.

"You're on TV," I said.

Carmen pulled off of me and turned around in time to see her picture.

"Authorities in Shasta County believe this woman to be the killer of carnival-owner Leonard Dupree, who was stabbed to death sometime last night in Garver. They also believe this woman to be the Sundown Killer, a serial killer who stalked the freeways in Tehama and Shasta Counties ten years ago. She is also believed to be the killer of a trucker spending the night in his cab at the Pantyhose Junction in Dunnigan."

"Son of a bitch," Carmen said. She breathed the words.

I smiled. "Wow," I said. "How about that, huh? I'm fucking a celebrity."

She turned to me with a dark look on her face. "You think it's funny?"

"A little, yes. The way you've been denying it to me."

"I haven't been denying it. I just haven't been admitting it."

"Why did you kill the trucker?"

For a moment, her beautiful face took on an ugly, fierce look. She clenched her teeth as she said, "Because the son of a bitch touched me, that's why. I told him I'd kill him if he touched me, and he touched me, anyway, so I did."

I reached over and took her arm, pulled her toward me. I put my arm around her shoulders and said, "You know, you can't just go around doing that, Mattox. I mean, it's against the law and everything."

"I was doing the world a favor," she said. "Every single time."

"That's very possible, but the police don't think that way."

"They all touched me. I hitched up and down the freeways, and one after another, they'd pick me up and they'd try to touch me, they all wanted to touch me."

"Hey, you're very touchable."

She turned to me with that fierce look and it created a cold splash in my chest. For that moment, I could see it in her eyes, the ability to kill. No, more than that. The desire. It opened wide in her eyes for that brief moment. Then it disappeared and she looked sad. "You think I had it coming?" she whispered.

"No, no, I'm not saying that. I'm just saying you can't go around killing every guy who tries to touch you. What were you doing hitchhiking, anyway?"

"I had nowhere to go. I was homeless. So I just hitched up and down the freeway. At night. At night, when the sun went down, I hit the freeway. That's why they called me the Sundown Killer, 'cause I only did it at night. And I didn't do it every night, 'cause I was afraid they'd catch me. And one after another, they picked me up. And they tried to touch me."

She said nothing and stared at her lap for a while. I saw a teardrop fall from her eye and I pulled her close, turned her head and kissed her.

"Hey," I whispered, "where were we?"

She threw a leg over my thighs and settled down on my cock.

"About here," she said as she began to move on me.

We looked into each other's eyes silently for a while. When we finally spoke, it was in whispers.

"Why did you cut yourself on the leg last night?" I said.

"To explain the blood on my clothes. I figured you'd see it."

"What about the trucker. How did you find his truck?"

"When he left, I went to the restroom, remember? Except I didn't go to the restroom. I followed him out to his truck."

After a long silence, I asked, "How many?"

She shrugged her shoulders and said, "I dunno. Ten. Twelve. Fifteen. Something like that."

"Because they tried to touch you? All of them?"

She nodded solemnly.

"You mean…you didn't enjoy it? The killing, I mean?"

Carmen frowned then and stopped moving for a moment.

I smiled. "Of course you did. Or you wouldn't have kept doing it. You enjoyed it, didn't you? It's okay, you can tell me. I know. Didn't you? Didn't you en—"

"Yes," she hissed, teeth clenched again. "Yes. I did." She trembled all over. "I did enjoy it. I did." Then she broke and started sobbing. She fell against me and cried on my shoulder.

I put my arms around her and just let her cry for a while. I was still inside her, and felt every sob down there. I reached over and turned off the TV.

"It's okay," I said finally. "You can't help it. I know. I know from experience."

"Can't help what?" she said, sniffling.

"You can't help that you like to kill, that you're compelled to do it and you're just looking for a reason. You can't help that."

"How…do you know?"

"I'll tell you later," I said. "Right now, let's get back to what we were doing, okay?"

She smiled in spite of her teary, puffy eyes and moved up and down on me, her hands on my shoulders. Our eyes never left each other.

"You know what it's like," she whispered after a few minutes.

I nodded.

"Then that means…you're…a killer."

I nodded again.

She smiled, squeezed me with her pussy. Then she went wild on me, laughing as she pounded me hard. I was ready to do some pounding myself, so I rolled her over on her back. She laughed as we finished up, and kept laughing as I rolled off of her. She sat up next to me and crossed her legs.

"Benedetti, I think you and I—I think we were meant to be," she said, then she laughed some more.

Chapter 7

We went into the nearest town and found a drugstore where Carmen bought some hair coloring, a pair of weak reading glasses, and a pair of scissors. We stopped at a liquor store and bought a bottle of good scotch. Back at the motel, Carmen put a chair at the mirror just outside the bathroom and began to cut her hair.

"I'm sorry to see it go," I said. "It's beautiful hair."

"Don't worry," she said, "it'll grow back fast."

Ninety minutes later, she had short, wavy blonde hair and wore glasses. The effect was substantial. She did not look at all like herself.

I unwrapped the two drinking glasses by the sink, opened the bottle, and poured for both of us. We took a few swallows as we sat on the edge of the bed.

She took my glass from me, put our drinks on the nightstand, then pushed me back on the bed and said, "Let's see if blondes have more fun."

That night, we found a steakhouse to celebrate her new look with a couple of rib-eyes. We were seated in a back booth in the dimly-lighted restaurant, with a candle guttering in a red glass bowl in the center of the table, where we ordered cocktails and were given menus.

"When we get to L.A.," she said, "will you take me to Disneyland?"

"I'll take you anywhere you want to go," I said. "I'll show you all the sights."

Our waitress was young and chewed gum. I noticed the chips in her burgundy nail polish as she set our drinks on the table. I thanked her.

"We really should hit the road again after dinner," I said. "It's just a couple more hours away."

Somehow, I felt if we could get to my place okay, then everything would be okay. I don't know where that feeling came from. It was absurd, of course.

We sat on opposite sides of the booth and both leaned forward so we were close over the candle.

"So," I whispered, "I'm having dinner with the Sundown Killer."

Carmen smiled in golden candlelight, and she looked beautiful in a sexy, sophisticated way, like the women in liquor ads. A shot of her sitting there, drink in hand, enjoying her favorite scotch, would sell a lot of bottles.

"What do they call you?" she said.

"What does who call me?"

"I dunno. The press?"

"The press doesn't know I exist."

"What're you, like, the mob? The Mafia, is that what we're talking about?"

"I've worked for mob guys before," I said with a nod. "But I'm not Mafia. Never was. I was always an independent contractor. Some contracts, they wanted the very best, so they came to me. One guy I did a couple jobs for, he called me Bullseye."

"Why?"

"Because I always got the job done perfectly. In other words, I always hit the bullseye."

"Bullseye's better than the Sundown Killer."

"Are you really a serial killer?"

She got a funny, squirmy look on her face. "Do we have to talk about me?"

"I think I have a right to know as much as I can about you. How do I know you won't stab me to death in my sleep?"

Carmen looked wounded. She sat back in the booth and placed a hand over her chest. "How can you say that, Benedetti?" she said. "I told you—" She sat forward again. "Remember when I told you that I liked it when you stared at my breasts?"

I nodded.

"That may not seem like much to you, but it means a lot to me. Because they're stared at all the time by people I don't want to stare at them. But when you stare at them…when it's you, I'm not ashamed of them, I don't want to hide them. When you stare at them, I feel proud of them. When I told you that…it was a big deal for me. I mean, for me, it's like saying 'I love you.' How could you think I'd ever want to hurt you? How *could* you?"

I reached over and took her hand. "I'm sorry. Come on, let's look at these menus. I don't know about you, but I'm hungry." She smiled. "I'm starving."

After dinner, we went back to the motel and got our things together. Carmen insisted on a quicky before we left.

In the car, she found a radio station that played music from the eighties, and we sang "Vacation" together along with the Go-Gos.

We drove on like that for a while, singing along with the songs on the radio. Then Carmen turned down the volume, unfastened her seatbelt, and knelt in her seat facing me.

"What made you a good hitman?" she said.

"Nobody ever knew who the hell I was," I said with a smile. "They still don't. I'm as good at staying invisible as I am at the rest of the job. Carmen, listen to me. I've got to tell you this. I'm not…I've never, uh…I'm not very good at conveying my emotions to other people. I usually keep them to myself. I haven't been in anything remotely resembling a relationship in at least ten years, and I've never been in one that lasted all that long. I'm kind of a…a loner, I guess."

"What's your point?" She began poking me in the ribs with her fingers and said, "What's your point, Benedetti, huh? Come on, whatcherpoint, whatcherpoint?"

I laughed because I was ticklish. "Not when I'm driving, dammit, not when I'm—stop it!" She stopped and I kept looking at her as I drove. "I'm trying to be serious, here, believe it or not." It was hard to stop smiling, though. "Earlier, while you were sleeping, I was thinking about my retirement. It's something I've been thinking about a lot over the past year. I've got all these things I wanted to do after I retired, places I wanted to go, things to see. I thought I was enthused about it. But then I thought, now I'm going to do them with Carmen, and I realized I hadn't been enthused about those plans at all. I'd been…well, kind of dead inside. But now, I'm happy, for the first time in…a long time. I can honestly say I'm happy. Because you're coming home with me." She rushed forward to kiss me, and I held up my right arm and laughed and said, "No, no, not while I'm driving."

Carmen took my hand and kissed the palm, then pressed it to the side of her face. "You don't know what it's been like for me, either. To know I make you happy…and that you appreciate me…you just don't know what that means to me." She kissed my hand again. "And on top of all that…you're loaded!"

We both laughed.

"Would you please get in your seat and put on your seatbelt," I said.

She sighed as she sat down and fastened her belt. "How much longer?"

"Another twenty minutes or so, is all."

"You mean…we're here?"

"Yep, we're here."

At my place, I parked in the garage, got out, and carried our bags inside. I turned on lights as I went through the house.

"You have a beautiful place," she said.

"Thank you. It's big enough for me and my dog and cat. I have a cleaning woman comes in twice a week and cleans up after me."

I went out on the porch and was greeted by my mutt Baxter, who barked as he jumped up and put his forepaws on my legs. I petted him and let him lick my face a little.

I gave Carmen a quick tour of the house, fed Baxter and my cat Leopold, and the whole time, she kept smiling as if someone had just told her she'd won the lottery. When I was done, she kissed me and said, "You know what? We're gonna have to fuck in each one of these rooms."

I laughed and said, "Sounds good to me. The house has never gotten a proper breaking in."

I told her to unpack her bag in one of the guest rooms if she wanted a place of her own for her stuff. She took her bag upstairs. I went up right behind her with my bag. In my bedroom, I took off my clothes and put on a blue robe over my boxers. Downstairs, I went to the liquor cabinet in the dining room and put the bottle of whisky we'd bought on a shelf. I poured some for Carmen. I mixed up some vodka and crème de cacao in a shaker and poured myself a vodka stinger.

Carmen came downstairs in an enormous black T-shirt that almost came to her knees.

"How about some TV?" I said.

We took our drinks into the living room and I turned on the television. We sat down on the couch. As I flipped through the channels with the remote, Carmen lay back and put her head on my lap.

"Tell me," I said, "when did you start killing?"

She said nothing for a long time, and I just kept channel surfing.

Finally, she said, "When I was a little girl."

"Animals?"

"Bugs first. Then animals. There was...I don't know, something about making them die, it made me feel so...I don't know, so..."

"Powerful?"

I felt her nod against my thighs. "Yeah. Powerful."

"Can you give it up?"

"What?"

"The killing. Can you give it up?"

Carmen sat up beside me, turned to me. "What do you mean, give it up?"

"I mean, can you stop? See, because with me, it's not compulsive. I can take it or leave it. I mean, it's…it's an ability I have, not a need. But you…I think it's a little different with you. Am I right?"

She frowned down at her lap for a while, looking a little lost.

"Is that asking too much?" I said.

She still said nothing.

"I mean, I'm retired now. I don't want any trouble. If we're going to be together, you can't be going around killing people."

"That…that was one of Lenny's conditions, too," she said. "That I stop. And I did."

"Oh. Well." I took a deep breath and let it out slowly. "If it's any consolation, it's my only condition. Who knows, maybe while we're together, you won't want to." I smiled at her. "I intend to keep you pretty occupied."

She leaned over and kissed me. "Care to start by breaking in the living room?"

Chapter 8

The rest of that summer was, hands down, the best time of my life.

Carmen and I hardly held still for a moment. When we weren't fucking like rabbits, we were out doing something—seeing movies or plays or concerts, eating out, dancing, visiting a museum or two, wandering through the zoo. We did all the touristy stuff. We walked down Hollywood Boulevard and looked at the stars in the sidewalk, visited the Hollywood Wax Museum, saw a movie at the Chinese Theater, toured Universal Studios. We spent two whole days in Disneyland and stayed the night at the hotel there.

Wherever we went, we were like high school kids in love. We couldn't keep our hands off of each other and we kissed often, held hands a lot. It felt good to be with her, to watch her enjoy herself. It felt good to be seen with her, this movie-star gorgeous blonde.

I took a lot of Viagra.

Some nights, we rented old movies and made slow love on the couch as they played on television, the grey light from the screen pulsing on our naked bodies. Then we got drunk and fell asleep together on the couch.

Then one night in late September, we were having sex on the bed when Carmen said something that bothered me a little.

"I cut Lenny's throat from behind first," she said between gasps. I was going at it pretty hard, and each time I slammed into her, her voice hitched from the impact. "That made him drop onto the couch. In his trailer. And I knelt down in front of him. And I started to stab him. Everything…everything came back up…our whole relationship…everything he ever did to piss me off…to hurt me…everything…and I just kept stabbing and stabbing."

"Like you did the others, the freeway killings."

The conversation ended there.

"Oh, you're doin' it, Benedetti, you're doin' it to me," she said, panting. "Let me roll over."

We rolled over so she was on top, and she rode me wildly until we finished off. A little later, I lay on my back beside her and she nestled in my arm, put a leg over my legs.

"Benedetti," she whispered.

"Hm?"

"Look at me."

I turned my head and looked at her as she looked up into my eyes.

"These months with you," she said, "they're the best I've ever had in my life."

"I'm glad."

"No one's ever…done things like this with me, y'know? All the guys I've dated, they kept me at home, didn't take me out or nothin'. Sometimes I wondered if they were ashamed of me."

"Carmen, you need to hang with a better class of people," I said. "And I intend to see that you do."

"You're going to introduce me to all your friends?"

"Well…to be honest, I don't have a lot of friends."

"Tell me, Benedetti, have the last few months been fun for you, too?" she said.

"The best of my life, Carm," I said. "The very best. But we're just getting started, you know. You're talking like you have to go back to college next week, or something."

She sat up on the bed and crossed her legs, facing me. I took off my condom and tossed it into a small waste basket on the other side of the nightstand.

"I'm…I'm having, um, a kind of…problem," she whispered.

"What's that?" I said.

She leaned toward me and took my hand. "I'm…missing it. I'm missing it bad."

I said nothing, just stroked her hand with my thumb.

She said, "Don't you miss it sometimes? Just a little?"

I shook my head. "Carmen, that part of the job…the actual killing…that wasn't my favorite part. It was the pursuit that I enjoyed. The actual killing…I didn't really feel one way or the other about it at the time. I was indifferent to it. What made me good at what I did was that I could do it, and it didn't bother me."

"Then why did you quit?"

"I just decided…enough was enough."

"And you don't miss it?"

"Not the killing."

She chewed what little was left of a fingernail on her right hand. "I know they're out there. It drives me nuts. I know they're out there, driving around, just waiting for some woman to come along. Or some girl. Anything they can stick it into. They're out there and there's nothing I can do about it."

I said, "Well, look at it this way—it's not your responsibility. Your only responsibility is to live your life, and to make it as pleasant as possible. Those guys out on the freeways—they're none of your concern, you got that, Mattox?"

The corners of her mouth rose, but it was a pale ghost of her usual smile. She looked sad, a little lost.

"Is there anything I can do to make you feel better?" I said.

"Hold me?"

I held out my arms for her. She lay down and put her head on my chest.

"You know," she said, "to make sure I don't make any mistakes and get caught, you could always…teach me."

"*Teach* you? Teach you what?"

"How to kill…without getting caught."

I chuckled.

She pulled away and propped herself up on an elbow. "I'm serious, you could teach me. Then we'd both be happy. I'd be able to do what I like to do once in a while, and you wouldn't have to worry about me getting caught."

I shook my head. "There are no guarantees that you won't get caught. The fact that I've never been caught has as much to do with luck as any skill on my part. I could teach you everything I know, and you could go out the next day and get nailed. It means nothing."

Carmen closed a hand around my flaccid penis and put her face close to mine. "I have to kill someone soon, Benedetti. I have to see the fear and the life drain out of someone's eyes. I have to hear that final rattle in someone's throat. You kill people for a living and you tell me you don't miss those things?"

"I don't miss them because they mean nothing to me."

"Try to understand, then."

"I killed the people I killed because someone paid me a lot of money to do it. Most of the people who pay me to kill are such scum, I always assume that anyone who would become involved with them in the first place probably deserves to die, anyway. But as far as the act itself, the killing alone—that does nothing for me. So, no, I'm sorry, but I can't understand."

"Please, Benedetti…"

"How long did you stop doing it for Lenny? Huh?"

She let go of my cock and flopped onto her back on the bed, put her right forearm across her forehead. "He thought I wasn't," she said. "But he couldn't keep track of me every second."

"You kept killing even after you told Lenny you'd stopped?"

"That's right."

"And he never found out?"

"Nope."

"Are you saying you're going to go on killing behind my back?"

After a long pause, she said, "If I have to."

I sighed. I couldn't have her running around at night killing people while I was asleep. My only sensible option would have been to stop seeing her, cut her off.

But I was addicted to Carmen, to the contours of her body, the smoothness of her skin, the way she laughed while we had sex—such joyous, happy laughter. I was even addicted to her low, smoky voice, to the way she said, "You're doin' it to me, you're doin' it to me," when she came. I loved the way she smelled and tasted. Everything about her had become a part of me in the short time we'd been together.

I couldn't cut her loose.

But the alternative…

"What are you thinkin' about?" she said.

"Just…thinking."

She sat up on her side of the bed, her back to me, and took a couple of swallows of her drink on the nightstand. She lit a cigarette and took a deep drag, blew the smoke out. Head bowed, she said, "It's somethin' I gotta do, Benedetti. I'm sorry. I can't help it."

I went across the bed to her, kissed the back of her neck.

"Okay," I said with a sigh. "I'll help you."

Chapter 9

I did something I should have done as soon as we got back to Los Angeles, but I was too busy having incredible sex: I took Carmen to see Rat-Face Charlie. He had a dingy little house in San Pedro.

Rat-Face Charlie was always in a hurry, as if he were always late for something, like Lewis Carroll's White Rabbit. He'd deal with you, but he'd rush you through. Even so, he was one of the best in town, maybe in the country. I'd called ahead and made an appointment. We showed up a few minutes early, because he always appreciated that.

"Steven, my friend," Charlie said when he opened the front door. He had not changed in the two years since I'd last seen him. He was tall and skinny, in his fifties, with greying brown hair he combed straight back, and a set of buck teeth that should have been fixed years ago. His face was pointy and rat-like, hence the name. He had a splotchy mustache, mostly white now, and his upper lip twitched occasionally. He wore brown loafers, tan slacks, and a yellow shirt. He opened his long skinny arms, and we embraced briefly. "It's been too long. How are you?"

"Just fine, Charlie," I said. "This is my friend. She needs an identity."

"Well, you come to the right place, then," Charlie said. "Let's go out back to the shed. Can I get you something to drink? I have ice-cold beer."

A cold beer sounded good, so I said yes. Charlie led us through the kitchen to a large dining area with a fully-stocked bar back in the corner.

"Step up to the bar," Charlie said.

There were three leather-upholstered stools at the bar, and Carmen and I sat on two of them. Charlie liked to talk before doing business. He was very sociable. The second he started working, though, he became hurried and flustered. Until then, he just wanted to drink and talk.

Charlie took three bottles of beer from the small refrigerator behind the bar, cracked them open, and poured them into glasses. "How's life treating you, Steven?" he said.

"I can't complain," I said.

We made small talk for a while as we drank our beers.

"Who's your friend, Steven?" Charlie said.

"Someone who needs a new identity," I said.

"I see." He smiled at Carmen. "And what's your name?"

"None of your business, Charlie," I said.

"Okay, I see, it's like that. All right. Bring your beers with you. Let's get this over with, I haven't got all day."

Charlie came out from behind the bar, and Carmen and I followed him into the kitchen, and out the back door. He had a spacious, well-tended back yard, with a brilliantly-colored flower garden in one corner.

In a back corner of the yard stood a square, grey, flat-roofed cinderblock building. There was a single window, blocked by a window-mounted air conditioner.

He took a ring of keys from his pocket and unlocked the three locks on the door. It was messy and cluttered inside, and hot. Charlie went to the air conditioner and turned it on.

The small building was divided by a wall into two rooms. The door in that wall had a red lightbulb mounted above it. The light was not on. There was a desk with two chairs in front of it, a grey metal file cabinet in the corner. The desk was covered with papers and manila folders. There was a goose-neck lamp on the desk covered with yellow, scribbled-on Post-It notes. On the other side of the room, a camera was mounted on a tripod facing a square of grey backdrop on the wall.

"C'mon, now," Charlie said, "let's get this done and over with, boring part first."

We sat in the chairs in front of the desk, facing Charlie, who shuffled through the mess before him. When he found what he wanted—a particular manila folder—he opened it. Pen in hand, Charlie asked Carmen several questions—he got all the necessary information from her and wrote it down as she recited it: sex, height, weight, eye color, that sort of thing.

"Okay, c'mon," Charlie said when he was done with the questions, "let's go, it's picture time, let's go."

He stood and led her over to the grey backdrop on the wall, told her where to stand. He got behind the camera and turned on the lamp. He took a few pictures, and that was it.

"It'll be a few days," Charlie said. "Okay, c'mon, let's wrap this up." He went over and turned off the air conditioner.

"How much do I owe you, Charlie?" I said as we left the small cinderblock building.

"We'll work that out in a few days, when you come get your merchandise," Charlie said.

"Are you sure?" I said. "I've got money in the car, I'm prepared to pay you."

Charlie shrugged as we crossed the lawn going back to the house. "Okay, let's say you pay me half today."

When he told me what "half" amounted to, I had to clench my teeth to keep my jaw from dropping. His prices had gone up and he was more expensive than I'd anticipated, but he was worth it. I went out to the car parked in front of his house, and I took a briefcase from the trunk. I opened it, took what I needed, and closed it again. I went back in the house and handed a couple of banded stacks of money to Charlie.

"I'll give you a call when it's ready," Charlie said.

I gave him my cell phone number before we left.

Three days later, Carmen became Lydia Streeter of Oklahoma City, Oklahoma.

She was still Carmen to me, but I trained myself to call her Lydia. Carmen was now someone out there, someone being pursued by the police. Lydia Streeter, with her short blonde hair and glasses, was not even on the radar, as far as the police were concerned.

"Lydia Streeter," she whispered to me as she lay on top of me that night, moving slowly up and down on me. "I'm a whole new person. And you gave that to me." She kissed me deeply and squeezed me down below. "Thank you, Benedetti."

My arms were around her and I stroked the back of her head. "You like having a new identity?"

"Hell, yeah! It's like…I get to start over again. I get to start over with you. Maybe I won't fuck up this identity the way I did the last one. Y'know?"

We kissed for a while and said nothing.

She squeezed me and whispered, "When are we gonna do it, Benedetti? Huh? I'm gettin' *real* impatient."

I said nothing, and after several seconds, Carmen—*Remember*, I thought, *it's Lydia now*—stopped moving, sat up a little and looked down at me.

"You said you would help me," she said.

"Yes, I did. And I will. But I'm very nervous about this, Carm—Lydia. I wanted to stay clean now that I'm retired. I wanted to put all the killing behind me."

"If you don't help me, I'll do it myself," she said.

"I know. That worries me even more, which is why I'll help you. At least then I'll know there's less chance of you getting nailed for it."

She squeezed me as she smiled. "What're you gonna teach me, huh? I'm very eager to learn, Mr. Benedetti. Do I have to bring you an apple, or will *this*—" She squeezed me again. "—do?"

She made me smile.

"Tell me about your work," she said.

"What about it?"

"Tell me a story. Tell me about one of your jobs. Give me all the details."

"Are you serious?"

"Yep. Let's hear it. Or I'll let you go limp inside me."

"I don't think I could go limp inside you," I said with a smile.

She started sliding up and down on me again. "C'mon, let's hear it. Tell me about somebody you killed. Tell me everything. Everything."

So I told her a story. As I spoke, I sometimes stopped to take a breath, because she was fucking me while I was talking, and it was difficult to concentrate.

"I once killed a man while he was throwing a party," I said. "He'd pissed off some business associates and they had decided to hire me. Beyond that, I know none of the details. The target was a man named William Styleswright. I didn't believe that name for a second, but it was the only one I had. Styleswright had a reputation for throwing great parties. I just showed up and went inside and joined the fun."

"Didn't you wear a disguise, or something?" she said.

"Yes, I did, come to think of it. I was sporting one of those rub-on tans out of a can, I had blond hair, a fake mustache, and glasses. I wore an Armani suit I'd bought specifically for that party. I looked like such an asshole, I didn't want to step outside the house. But that's what I was going for. I wanted to look like a typical Hollywood asshole, because I figured there would be a lot of them at the party and I would blend in. Who would remember one Hollywood asshole from another at a party in Malibu? The parked cars were thick up and down the street. I found a spot a good distance from the house and walked."

I stopped talking for a while and thrust up with my hips, biting my lower lip as I pushed into her repeatedly.

"Yeah?" she said. "Go on."

"I...I can't tell you a story a-and...and fuck at the same time, I'm sorry, I just can't."

She laughed then—more of a giggle, really—and started moving fast and hard on top of me, squeezing those muscles on the downstroke. She smiled down at me as my mouth opened wide and, before I could say another word, I exploded.

Lydia leaned forward with a big smile, kissed me, and said, "I love a man who comes when I want him to."

I laughed.

"Now," she said as she got off me. She lay down on her back beside me. "I want you to work me with your hand while you talk."

I was more than happy to comply. I lay down between her legs, propped my right elbow up on her thigh, and began to rub her slowly and gently with one hand.

She put a hand on top of my head and said, "Sweetie? Look, I get what you're trying to do, but you don't have to 'cause I'm already hot and bothered. So feel free to just get busy down there, okay?"

I had to laugh at her candid, honest suggestion.

As I got busy with my hands, I went on with my story.

"I had to get my host alone, for just a short time," I said. "It turned out to be a lot harder than I expected. He was constantly the center of attention. The man was like an overgrown attention-hungry child. That much was obvious about him immediately. I mingled and chatted." I smiled. "I told people I was a producer and I had a script I was really trying to see through to the end. Some of them were actually interested and asked what the script was about. I came up with some elaborate science-fiction blockbuster idea that sounded about as stupid as anything else that ends up in the multiplex, and several people gave me their cards.

"'Call me at my office,' one man said. 'I'd like to read that script, uh…what did you say it was called?'

"'*Hammerblow*,' I said, off the top of my head.

"'Ah, that's a hot title,' the guy said. 'Sounds like the kinda thing that makes big bucks overseas.'

"I swear, if I'd wanted to, and if I'd really had a script, I think I could've gotten a movie made. But the whole time, I kept my eye on my man. When I saw him duck down a hallway, I worked my way through the group of partiers and followed him. He went down the hall to the room at the very end. His bedroom, it turned out. He went in and swung the door closed behind him, but it didn't close all the way. I tapped a knuckle on the door and pushed my way in. He spun around and wanted to know who I was. I told him I wanted to talk about a movie I was trying to get financed, and as I spoke, I moved closer to him, until I was close enough. I punched him in the face hard, and he went down."

As I talked, I fucked Lydia slowly with two fingers. She trembled and squirmed, but kept her eyes on me.

"I took the silenced .22 pistol from the small of my back under my shirt," I said, "and I put it to his eye and fired twice. I checked his pulse and made sure he was dead."

Lydia began to moan. "You killed him," she gasped. "You killed him, right?"

"Yep. Then I put the gun back under my shirt and rejoined the party. I stayed for another fifteen minutes, or so, then left."

"Fuck me."

"What?"

"I want you inside me now, fuck me." She sat up reached over and grabbed my cock and squeezed. I was instantly hard.

I got on top of her and entered her.

"Did he make a sound?"

"What do you mean?"

"When he died, when he died," she said impatiently. "Did he make a sound when he died?"

"I didn't wait around to find out," I said.

She clutched my back and said, "Harder. *Harder*."

I moved harder, but suddenly I was afraid of losing my erection. Seeing her get off on the details of a killing—it was disturbing. But she bucked and writhed, until she finally wrapped her arms and legs around me and whispered, "You're doin' it to me, Benedetti, you're doin' it to me." Then her entire body shuddered repeatedly as she grunted and gasped.

I began to see how much Lydia enjoyed what she did.

I began to see just how disturbed she was.

I wondered, once again, if it had been a mistake to take her in.

Then I looked down at her, lying naked beneath me, her pale body as luscious as some creamy dessert.

How big a mistake could it be? I wondered.

I'd find out. Eventually.

Chapter 10

We went out to breakfast the next morning. I took her to a little mom-and-pop greasy-spoon I liked, one of the few left. It was the kind of mom-and-pop place that's become so hard to find in the jungle of sterile, corporate chains. It was run by Mr. and Mrs. Koulouris, Greek immigrants with two daughters, Anna and Theresa, who helped out in the diner when they weren't in school. Mr. and Mrs. Koulouris spoke iffy English with heavy accents, while their two lovely daughters were accent-free and thoroughly Americanized. Mr. Koulouris sometimes complained to me that his girls, both American-born, had no respect for tradition.

Mr. Koulouris greeted us and directed us to a booth, gave us menus. It was a small diner with Formica-topped tables between blue, vinyl-upholstered benches. We ordered omelettes when Anna came with her order pad. She poured coffee for us, then left.

We leaned close and whispered to each other.

"You can't just go around killing people," I said. "Especially the way you're doing it."

"Then how should I do it?" Lydia slipped a bare foot between my thighs.

"You're doing it the same way each time. The cops recognize your work. Right away, you're at a disadvantage. You do it differently each time, the killings can't be connected."

"Is that how you do it?"

"The method I used—" I smiled when I felt her foot. "Please stop that," I whispered.

"Mm," she said as she pulled her foot away. "All business."

"This is serious. If you want to do this right, you have to be all business about it."

"That's because for you, it was business. For me, it's…different."

"Yeah, I know it's different for you. But that doesn't change anything. You still want to do it right, don't you?"

She nodded as she ran her foot up the inside of my leg.

"You never stop, do you?" I said with a smile.

She smiled. "You know what the problem with you is, Benedetti?"

"What?"

"Your mind isn't dirty enough. You need a dirtier mind. By the time I'm done with you, your mind is going to be filthy."

"I don't want you to be done with me," I said.

"Just a figure of speech, Benedetti. Don't worry. I'll never be done with you."

My smile did not move, but her last sentence echoed in my mind. Something about it didn't quite sit well with me. It had an ominous tone that Lydia did not intend.

"We're doing this now, okay?" I said. "I need you to concentrate. This is important. If we're going to do this, we're going to do it my way."

"Okay, boss." She took her foot away. "Teach me."

"As I was saying, " I said, but I waited as Anna came with our omelettes. She set the plates down and I thanked her, and she went away. We ate as we talked in low tones and whispers. "As I was saying, the method I used depended entirely on the circumstances. I would tail my target for a while, get to know his routine, the places he went. I made note of the times, everything. Then I tried to figure out when he was most vulnerable. Then I decided on the safest, quickest, easiest, and most effective way of doing him."

"Like a silenced .22 pistol," she said.

I nodded. "That was one way. Sometimes I used a knife, sometimes I strangled or smothered them. The method had to be, as the kids say these days, organic. It had to grow from the circumstances so that, in a way, it would be a part of the circumstances. Does that make sense?"

She nodded. "So you're saying you want me to tail someone for a while?"

"If you want to do this right."

"What's the alternative?"

I shrugged. "I suppose you could go to a bar, pick up some guy, go to a motel, and do him there."

She smiled. "Yeah, that's more my speed."

I sighed. "All right, then you go to a bar you've never been to in a city you've never visited, and you...do it."

"Can we do it tonight?"

"I don't see why not."

"Good." She bounced a little on her bench. "Oh, I can't wait. You'll be there, won't you?"

"Well, I'll be close by."

"Good, I want you close by. I want you with me, if possible."

"Here's how it'll go. We'll go, uh...to the Valley. Yeah, we'll find a bar in the Valley, one with a motel near by. I'll park.

You'll go inside. I'll wait a while, and I'll go in after you. I'll be there watching while you…well, pick whoever you want to…be with. But you and I won't talk or anything, it's important no one thinks we're there together."

"If it's important no one thinks we're there together, then why are you going to be there?"

"I'm a pretty quick study when it comes to people," I said. "I'm not sure I trust your judgment. If you choose someone I think will be trouble, I'll step in. Barring that, though, you tell your target there's a motel just up the street, you want to go there. You go out with him. I'll follow you out. He'll take you over to the motel. I'll park on the street in front of the motel. Let him get the room, don't go in the office with him. You get in the room, make sure the door is unlocked. I'll be watching to see what room you go into. I'll give you time to…do what you need to do. The quicker you do it, the better. Then I'll come get you, make sure everything's okay."

"I want you there, in the room," she said with quiet urgency.

"I'll be there, don't worry. Then we'll calmly walk to the car and drive away. Then it would probably be a good idea to dye your hair again. Don't wear your glasses into the bar."

"Why not?"

"Then later, when the cops are asking questions, the bartender, and anyone else in the bar who sees you, won't describe you as a woman wearing glasses. When you're done, you go back to wearing the glasses."

"Do you think they look sexy on me?" she said as she pushed her glasses up on her nose.

"Lydia, a duck suit would look sexy on you."

We finished our breakfast and drove back to my place. Lydia took off her clothes and dropped them to the living room floor, then flopped down on the couch.

"Come fuck me," she said.

She was insatiable. She never stopped.

Afterward, I lay on my back on the couch with Lydia stretched out on top of me, both of us naked.

"Thank you for doing this, Benedetti," she whispered, her head resting on my shoulder. "I mean, you don't have to do this for me, and I just want you to know I appreciate it."

"I'm only doing it for one reason," I said as I stroked her back. "I know I haven't known you long, but…I honestly don't think I could live without you. That's why I'm doing it."

She raised her head and looked into my eyes. "Really?" she said. The word was little more than a breath.

I nodded.

Lydia kissed me deeply. When she pulled back, she whispered, "Nobody's ever said anything like that to me before. Nobody's ever been this good to me, Benedetti. Ever."

"I'm afraid I just don't understand the man who wouldn't move earth for you if you asked him to."

"You're a great guy, Benedetti, but I've got news for you," she said. "You're about as rare as snowstorms in the desert. Most men are shits. They deserve what they get from me."

"Well, I'm not going to apologize for my gender."

"No, I don't expect you to. You're different, Benedetti. You're not like them. My guess is, you had a good mother."

"I did," I said.

"She raised you right. You're a gentleman, you're kind, you're passionate." Her eyes sparkled as she smiled at me. "Yeah, Benedetti, your mom raised you right."

If Mom only knew.

"Gotta go to the little girls' room," Lydia said as she got up.

I noticed she'd left her purse on the floor nearby.

Lydia *never* left her purse unattended. She didn't let that thing out of her sight. I'd been wanting a look. I was curious to see what kind of weapon she carried.

I got up and reached for the purse—but I pulled my hand back and sat down again.

I was struck by an early memory, and something that had been pounded into my head throughout my childhood. I must have been four, maybe even three. I decided to see what Mom had in her purse. I started pulling stuff out and putting it on the floor beside me: keys, a notebook, a wallet, a checkbook, a change purse. Before I got any further, Mom caught me in the act.

She slapped the back of my hand a couple of times, and said, "Stevie, you never, *ever* get into a lady's purse without permission. Do you understand? *Never*. A lady's purse is *very private.*"

Thanks to Mom, I think by the time I was five, I was afraid of women's purses.

I reached for Lydia's purse again, but pulled back quickly when I heard the downstairs bathroom door open down the hall. She hadn't taken long. I wondered if it was because she realized she'd left her purse behind.

She sat down on the couch next to me. "Believe it or not," she said, "I missed you."

"I thought of nothing but you while you were gone," I said with a smirk.

She laughed and said, "We're about to make me puke."

―――――――――

Later, I drove into the San Fernando Valley and got on Ventura Boulevard in Studio City.

"You look for bars," I said, "and I'll look for motels."

"There's a bar over here," she said, pointing.

"I don't see any motels close by."

We drove on, looking. I saw a couple of motels, but there were no nearby bars.

Finally, in Sherman Oaks, we found the Carriage House, a small hole-in-the-wall bar a couple doors down from the Starlite Motel.

"This is it," I said. "It's perfect."

"Do we go in and look around?"

"No."

"Okay. Then what do we do?"

"Kill time until tonight, I guess."

She looked at me with the sexiest, most promise-filled smile I'd ever seen, and I knew what we would be doing for the rest of the afternoon.

After a romp in the bedroom, we went out back and got in the pool. She floated naked on her back, eyes closed, while I stood beside her in water up to my chest.

"You planning on having sex with this guy tonight?" I said.

She opened her eyes and smiled at me. "Why, Mr. Benedetti, are you *jealous*?"

"Maybe a little."

"No. Don't worry, I won't let him touch me. That would be…*sick*." She rolled over and faced me, wrapped her arms and legs around me. "Face it, Benedetti. You're stuck with me. It's never been like it is with you. Not even close. So don't worry. Nobody touches me but you. You can do anything you want. With me, to me. I'll never tell you no, Benedetti. Never." Her eyes were so solemn, her lips together in a straight line. Then she kissed me.

I had no idea how to respond to that. The silent alarm went off in the back of my head. I didn't ignore it, but I shied away from it. I didn't want there to be any alarms. I wanted so much for it to be that good, for it to work. I wanted it so bad that I let that alarm wear itself out with no response.

Chapter 11

That night around ten, we drove back into the Valley. It was a warm, sticky night. It was raining again—not very hard, little more than a sprinkle. I parked at the curb a couple of doors up from the Carriage House.

"Thank you so much for this," Lydia said. She leaned over and kissed me.

"I'll come in soon," I said. "But just ignore me."

She smiled and said, "Tonight when we get home, I'm going to fuck your brains out for this."

"Honey, it's a wonder I have any brains left."

She got out of the car and walked to the bar. She wore a tight, white middy blouse, a short black skirt that hugged her ass. Her long legs were bare all the way down to her black heels.

My god, she was a sight. I got an erection just watching her walk away, which wasn't all that pleasant because my cock was sore from the workout it had been getting. She disappeared into the bar.

I checked my watch.

Ten minutes later, I went in. I stood just inside the door and sized up the place.

The curved bar was to the right. On the left, there was a row of four booths up against the wall, a few more in the back. To my immediate right were two small tables along the wall. I sat at the one closest to the bar, my back to the door. Normally, I didn't like to sit anywhere with my back to the door, but it was the only way I could watch Lydia, who sat at the bar flanked by unoccupied stools. I'd expected her to be with someone already.

There were a few other people seated at the bar—two overweight, middle-aged women who talked quietly, a man in his sixties drinking alone, three fiftyish men talked and laughed with the bartender at the other end of the bar and a couple of the booths were occupied. I spotted a man in the farthest of the four booths. Alone, in his late thirties, slim, bushy dark hair that looked like it hadn't seen a comb or brush in a while, and small wire-rimmed glasses. He looked like the artist type, maybe a musician, something like that. I noticed him because he stared at Lydia. He bowed his head for a few seconds, looked up at her, then down again.

I recognized all the signs—the knee bobbing nervously under the table, the rigid posture, the look of utter bafflement—and realized he was trying to muster the courage to go talk to her. It was something all men have in common, the act of stirring up the guts to approach a woman for the first time. It starts in our teen years, and we think we'll grow out of it, that it'll get easier when we're older. But it doesn't, not really. We just get better at masking our fear and insecurity, even from ourselves. Each time we approach a woman, we open ourselves to rejection, and with each rejection, a small part of us dies.

Of course, that nervous guy in the booth stood to lose considerably more than a small part of himself.

Apparently, the Carriage House was not an establishment that provided table service, so I stood and went to the bar. The bartender was a jovial, barrel-chested man of about forty or so with a florid complexion and a thick head of curly blond hair. I ordered a vodka stinger, paid for it, and took it back to my table.

I watched Lydia peripherally as I stared contemplatively into my drink.

It took a while longer, but the bushy-haired guy finally stood and went to the curved bar. He perched himself on the stool next to her, on the other side of her from me. From my table, I had a view of them both under the soft light above the bar.

Shaggy hunched his shoulders slightly as he spoke to her. He smiled and kept his eyes level with hers, although I'm sure they were being drawn downward by Lydia's cleavage.

Lydia returned his smile and said something to him, then tipped her glass back and finished her drink. Shaggy called the bartender over and ordered Lydia another drink, then he nodded toward his booth, where he had left his glass. The bartender came with her drink and Shaggy paid for it. Then they went to his booth together.

He sat facing me, but I could not see her on the other side of the divider. Shaggy smiled a lot, nodded while she spoke.

I watched and waited. Watching and waiting were major elements of the occupation from which I had just retired. The trick was to not *look* like I was watching and waiting. I'd gotten very good at that over the years.

Forty-five minutes passed.

I got a second drink.

An hour.

I'd expected her to pounce sooner. She came in at one hour and seven minutes.

They got up and left together, holding hands. I did not lift my head as they passed, but I saw it—their hands together between them—and a cold spear of jealousy pierced my chest.

I told myself I was being ridiculous, but it didn't matter. I even smiled a little at the tenacity of that jealousy.

I waited a few minutes, finished my drink, and left the bar. I went to my car and got in, drove up to the motel, and parked at the curb, engine idling. From my car, I could see the silver Toyota Camry parked beneath the portico. Lydia was in the passenger seat and Shaggy was in the office getting a room.

He looked so happy and excited as he came out and got back into the Camry. He was about to have sex with the beautiful woman in the car, he had reason to be happy and excited. As far as he knew.

I waited a few minutes, popped a couple of Tic Tacs into my mouth, then pulled away from the curb. As I slowly drove by the motel, I saw them getting into a ground-floor room. The Camry was parked directly in front of the room.

I accelerated and drove away from the motel. I went around the block a few times. I gave her ten minutes, then I parked in the same spot I'd left ten minutes ago, killed the engine, and got out of the car.

As I passed under the portico, I stopped at a newspaper vending machine and fished in my pocket for change. I saw no one at the desk in the office. I bought a paper, folded it over and tucked it under my left arm as I strolled on, my hands in my pockets. I bought the paper only because it looked good, it somehow made me look, to anyone who might be watching, like I belonged there. Another trick I'd picked up in my previous line of work.

As I walked to the room I'd seen them enter earlier, I wondered if she'd stuck to the plan. I hoped so. I hoped she hadn't left the Sundown Killer signature.

I went to the room—number 103—and opened the door, went inside.

She had told me she wouldn't take long. She had been right.

When I was nine, I saw a man get hit by a truck. Happened right in front of me. The man was crossing the street, and then he was part of the street. He seemed to come apart as he rolled beneath the tires, and he came out looking like nothing more than a bundle of meat. That memory stood out vividly; I could see it as clearly as if it had been yesterday. It was probably my ugliest memory. But as disturbing as that memory was, it had nothing on that motel room.

I quickly closed the door with the sickening feeling that I was on the wrong side of it.

Shaggy lay naked in the center of the bed, propped up against some pillows, legs spread, eyes and mouth open. She'd sliced him open from sternum to groin.

There was a lot of blood. She had cut his throat, and the arterial spray was bright on the headboard and wall.

On Lydia, too.

She was naked. At first, I thought she was wearing long gloves, but it was blood on her hands and forearms. One of her hands was between her legs. She straddled Shaggy's corpse on her knees, furiously masturbating with one hand while the other moved around inside him.

That's what it took for me to realize I had made a terrible mistake.

She saw me and bounded off the bed, rushed over to me, bloody hands reaching out to me.

I lifted my arms, palms out and said, "No, no, don't get that on me."

"Fuck me," she whispered. She reached for my hand, but I repeatedly pulled it away. "Please come fuck me now, Benedetti, right now, please."

"Get your clothes on," I said, my voice low.

"Please fuck me, Benedetti. Right now. On the bed. *Please.* Come over here." She reached for my hand again, and once again I kept it away from her. "*Goddammit,*" she growled, "do this for me, now, Benedetti, *please.*"

"I'm not fucking you here with all that blood on you," I said, quietly but firmly. "Now get your clothes on and let's get the hell out of here."

She dropped to her knees. "Please fuck me, Benedetti, please, right here, now, on the floor. Right here, please, you have to, please, fu—"

I swung my hand and slapped her hard. She fell to her side.

Lydia lay there, naked and bloodied, sobbing.

I bent down and picked her up by her upper arms, got her to her feet. I got some blood on my hands.

"You have to get *dressed,*" I said. "We have to *leave.*"

The sobs had passed and she took a deep breath, was able to focus a little better.

"Go wash your hands," I said. "Your clothes will cover most of the blood on you, but we can't go out there with blood all over your hands and arms like that. Go wash. But don't touch anything. Use a washcloth or something on the fixtures."

She nodded once and went to the bathroom. I heard the faucet running.

Her weapon—a hunting knife with a serrated edge—was on the bed beside Shaggy. Her purse was on the floor beside the bed.

How had I been so blind? Was I in love with her? Was that why I had ignored all my alarms? Was that why I had taken her in knowing she was a fucking serial killer?

Or was it just the fucking? I liked to think I was more sophisticated than that—than simply being ruled by my cock. That's what I liked to think.

Lydia came out of the bathroom with clean hands and arms. She got her clothes off the floor and put them on. Fortunately, they had been out of range of the spray of blood. She seemed weary, slow-moving. Her face seemed to droop—her eyes, the corners of her mouth. She did not meet my eyes as she came to my side, dressed and ready to go.

There was a smear of blood on her face, another on her flat belly between her blouse and skirt, nothing anyone would notice out there in the dark. I took her elbow and we left the motel room. I still had the newspaper tucked under my arm. We walked under the portico and turned left, went to my car and got in. I started the engine and pulled away from the curb.

Neither of us spoke for a long time. Lydia stared at her lap.

She finally whispered, "You wouldn't fuck me. Why? That's what I wanted. You said you'd do anything I wanted. It would've been so…perfect. If you had."

"You would've gotten blood all over me, and we'd both be a mess," I said. "And traditionally, it's a bad idea to leave DNA at the scene of a murder." I sounded calm, together, like nothing was bothering me. But something was bothering me. Just under my skin, where no one could see it, I had the shakes.

I could not lose the image of Lydia hovering bloodied over that sliced-open corpse, masturbating with a fierceness that showed on her face, a fierceness that peeled her lips back over her teeth and clenched her eyes shut beneath a deep frown. She hadn't looked like the same person. It was as if there had been some kind of animal inside her that emerged as she frantically fingered herself.

I sounded calm, but inside it was a different story.

After the more than two decades I'd been in my particular line of work, you'd think nothing would faze me. Hell, that's what I thought. But I felt sick to my stomach. I felt drained.

When I looked at Lydia on that drive home, I didn't see the same woman I'd seen before that night. Yes, she was still beautiful. But she was sick, twisted in a way I had not foreseen. I felt betrayed. She had led me to believe she was something she was not. I knew she was a killer, but there are killers…and then there are depraved monsters.

I saw her again in my mind, lying there straddling the corpse, getting herself off. I focused on both her hands. She'd had both hands inside him.

I imagined fucking her there, beside the corpse, bloody and panting, and my stomach turned.

She said nothing as I kept looking over at her. She didn't even lift her head.

I wondered what I was going to do with her. I certainly didn't want her around anymore, and there was no way I could have sex with her again. As I mulled the alternatives, red and blue lights flashed in my rearview mirror.

There was a police car behind me, and it was pulling me over.

Chapter 12

"Whatever you do," I said as I pulled over to the side of the road, "don't talk. Just be quiet. In fact, lean over on the door and pretend you're asleep. I'll take care of everything."

She did as I told her.

I popped a couple more Tic Tacs into my mouth. "Put your purse in your lap and cover up that smudge of blood on your stomach," I said.

She put the purse in her lap.

I took my wallet from my back pocket and removed my driver's license, then took the registration from the glovebox.

I rolled my window down in time to hear the door of the cruiser close. He took his time coming up to my window. The beam of his flashlight moved through the car, passed over me, briefly over Lydia.

"Evening," the cop said. "Can I see your license and registration, please?"

I heard the gentle rain pattering on his cap as I handed the license and registration to him through the window.

"Was I speeding?" I said with a smile.

"I'm afraid so, sir. Have you been drinking tonight?"

"No, I haven't. My wife and I just had dinner a little while ago, and she's not feeling well. I think she's having a bad reaction to the clams."

"Sit tight, I'll be right back."

The cop returned to his car. I looked over and saw Lydia slumped against the door.

I breathed a sigh of relief that the cop hadn't seen any of the blood on her when he'd shone his flashlight into the car.

A few minutes later, the cop returned to my window, handed me the license and registration, then filled out the ticket and told me to watch my speed. In a few minutes, I was back on the road. Neither of us spoke the rest of the way back to my place in Laurel Canyon.

I was lost in my own thoughts, which were unpleasant but necessary. By the time I reached my house, I knew what I had to do.

As soon as we got inside, Lydia said, "I'm taking a shower."

I went to the kitchen sink and washed my hands.

I went upstairs and found her on the way into the bathroom, naked.

"I have an errand to run," I said.

"This late?"

"Yeah. I'll be back in a while."

While she showered, I went out to the garage and got the shovel. I put it in the backseat of the Lexus. As I drove away, I saw the moon overhead between a couple of clouds. The rain had stopped, and great patches of stars were visible in the night sky.

———

I thought I was beyond being shocked by anything. I was wrong.

I couldn't eject from my mind the sight of Lydia kneeling over that corpse. It was not the beautiful woman I'd met at the carnival. It was some kind of deranged creature that seemed to emerge from inside the beautiful woman.

All those silent alarms in my head had been trying to warn me. That meant part of me, on some level, knew how dangerous she was, had known all along. But I'd gone ahead and taken her with me, anyway.

And I'd fallen for her, fallen hard.

As I drove that night, I knew that her sickness would never be cured. At the very least, she belonged in an institution. The cops were after her, which was reason enough to ditch her. The last thing I needed was a problem with the law.

I would miss her. I'd never met anyone like her before. She was so passionate and she had given me the best sex of my life.

But there was no hope for her. If the cops found her, she'd end up getting the death penalty. If they didn't find her, she'd go on killing men.

Poor Carmen, poor Lydia. She'd thought her new identity would give her a shot at a new life. It was a shame, really, her whole situation. I wished there was some other way, some way that would allow us to go on together. The last few months had been the best of my life—the best of hers, too, she'd said—and it caused a sharp pain in the pit of my stomach when I thought of never seeing her again.

But I had no choice.

When I got back three hours later, the house was dark. I assumed Lydia was in bed. My back and arms ached. I poured some vodka over a few ice cubes and drank. I took the bottle with me to the living room and turned on the TV.

I didn't feel like going to bed, although it was almost three in the morning. There was no way I was going to sleep with her. I'd sleep on the couch in front of the TV.

Turner Classic Movies was playing Dracula, the original with Lugosi, and I watched it as I drank and smoked a cigarette. I tried not to think too much. The vodka helped. Watching Dracula, however, did not. I found an old Danny Kaye movie instead.

When I started feeling sleepy, I took off my shoes and stretched out on the couch. It wasn't long before I drifted off to sleep.

As I slept, I dreamed of that bloody motel room, and when Lydia tried to wake me with a kiss, I reflexively pulled away from her and quickly sat up, expecting her to be naked and smeared with blood. She was not. She wore denim cut-offs and a white T-shirt with Daffy Duck on the front.

"Sorry," she said. "I didn't mean to scare you."

I ran my hand back through my hair. "I, uh…I was having a nightmare," I said.

"What would you like for breakfast? It's about quarter after nine. Would you like to sleep longer? I can leave you alone if you want."

"Um…" I stood and stretched. "Gimme a few minutes to wake up," I said. I went upstairs and undressed, took a shower. As I washed, I thought about what I was going to do and wondered if I'd be able to get Lydia to go along with it. Of course I would. She'd do anything I asked. That was what made it so difficult. She trusted me, had faith in me.

But it had to be done.

I looked out the bedroom window. It was sunny outside. There were a few scattered clouds, but it looked like the rain was over.

"Let's go on a picnic," I said when I entered the kitchen in jeans and a grey T-shirt tucked in under an unbuttoned pale-blue short sleeve shirt.

She was putting a pan on the stove and turned to me. "A picnic? Are you serious?"

"What, it doesn't sound like fun?"

She smiled. "Yeah. Sure."

"Great. I know a nice little place out in the desert. I've got a great picnic basket out in the garage. You can make some sandwiches, we'll take fruit, I've got some carrot cake left in the fridge. And we'll take a bottle of wine."

She said, "Boy, you're in a good mood today. I thought you'd...well, I figured you'd be..."

"What?"

"I don't know. Since you wouldn't do anything with me last night..."

"Let's talk about it over brunch, okay?"

She nodded. "Okay. I'll make sandwiches. Is tuna salad okay?"

"Yes. And there's some roast beef and cheese in the fridge."

I went out in the garage and got the wicker picnic basket. It was a big one, and included plates and utensils, linen napkins, two wine glasses, a corkscrew, and place to put the bottle in the deep wicker lid. I took it into the kitchen and put it on the table.

"Anything I can do to help?" I said.

"Nope, I've got it covered. Go watch TV, or something."

An hour later, I carried the basket out to the garage and put it in the back of my titanium-metallic Porsche Cayenne Turbo. Lydia came out after me with her purse slung over her shoulder. We got into the SUV and I opened the garage door. I backed out, went around the circular driveway and headed out.

The news was on and I quickly hit the Seek button. I didn't want to hear any news.

The ride seemed longer than it really was.

The radio played, and sometimes we sang along.

I got on Interstate 15 and headed toward Las Vegas. Just short of the California-Nevada border was a small town called Baker, and just south of Baker was a lush patch of desert called the Devil's Playground, which was where I was headed.

About fifteen minutes after I got off the freeway, Lydia said, "Where are we goin', exactly?"

"We're going to a piece of exquisite desert called the Devil's Playground. It covers thousands of acres with plenty of lush vegetation and all kinds of wildlife. It's beautiful."

"You like the desert?"

"I love it. As barren and empty as it looks sometimes, it's always full of life. When we get where we're going, we'll have our brunch, then I want to show you something."

She raised a brow. "Do I detect a bit of romance, Benedetti?"

I smiled. "If you want to think of it that way, sure."

Smiling was difficult. Everything was difficult. I couldn't believe I was being so upbeat and cheerful. I was torn up inside. It hurt to look at her, but I couldn't not look at her.

I got on a narrow, lonely road that snaked through the Devil's Playground: Kelbaker Road. The road's name was derived from its origin in Baker and its passage through the ghost town of Kelso. After a while, I turned the Cayenne off Kelbaker and onto a dirt road and picked up speed a little, kicking up a cloud of dust behind me. I drove on the dirt road for about fifteen minutes before the road disappeared. From then on, I had to avoid bushes and cacti, and lizards and field mice scurried out of the way ahead of me.

"How far is it?" she said.

"We're in the Devil's Playground now. Won't be much longer."

I turned up the radio when an AC/DC song came on. Lydia and I sang along with "Highway to Hell."

I drove for another fifteen minutes, farther and farther out into the desert.

I drove until I saw the red kerchief I'd hooked onto a branch of an enormous palo verde tree. I pulled up to the tree and stopped.

"See?" I said. "That palo verde gives us a nice spot of shade."

I got out and went to the back of the Cayenne. I opened it up and took out the old red blanket we'd brought with us, spread it out on the ground. I got the picnic basket and put it on the blanket.

"What's this thing you want to show me?" Lydia said as she sat on the blanket with her legs crossed.

I got down beside her and opened the basket. "We'll get to that. First, let's eat. I'm hungry."

I opened a bag of chips and unwrapped a roast beef sandwich. We said little as we ate, but we exchanged smiles. Those smiles made me feel guilty.

"You make a good sandwich," I said.

"I'm a woman of many talents," she said with a smile.

"You sure are."

She finished her sandwich as I opened the wine. I took the two wine glasses from inside the basket's lid and handed one to Lydia, then poured.

I raised my glass and said, "A toast. To…"

"To us, Benedetti," she said, then she touched her glass to mine.

It wasn't what I had in mind—not anymore—but she beat me to it. I sipped the wine.

"You'll never know, Benedetti," she said, "you'll just never, ever know how grateful I am to you. For what you've done for me."

I smiled.

She took my hand and kissed it. Holding it to her cheek, she said, "Promise you won't freak out when I say this?"

"I'm not the freaking out type," I said.

"I love you, Benedetti. I love you so much, I can feel it down in my toes." She got on her knees, came to me, and gave me a gentle, warm kiss. "You don't have to say anything, I don't expect you to. I just wanted you to know, Benedetti. I've…well, I've never felt this way about anyone. And I've never said those words to anyone. Not once. Not ever." She sat back down, legs crossed, and sipped her wine.

I didn't know what to say. Maybe it was best to say nothing. Maybe it was best to get this over with now before I lost my resolve.

It had to be done. I kept telling myself that over and over.

Why drag it out any longer than necessary? Who knew what she was going to say next, and I couldn't take any more of it. Saying she loved me—that was bad enough. It ripped my guts up. Made me feel like vomiting blood.

I stood. "Come here. I'll give you your surprise now."

"Oh, goodie!" she said as she got to her feet.

"Close your eyes," I said.

"What?"

"Close your eyes. Seriously. No peeking."

She closed her eyes and I put an arm around her shoulders and led her along. I took her around to the other side of the palo verde tree. I walked her over to the hole and stood her at the end of it, facing it. I took my arm away from her and stepped a couple of paces back.

"Okay," I said as I took my .45 from the small of my back in my right hand. I aimed it at her. "You can open them now."

From behind, I saw her head turn left and right, looking for something. Then, finally, she looked down. She saw the grave before her, the pile of dirt beside it on the right.

Lydia spun around and faced me. Her eyes were wide, her mouth open.

"No," she said. "No, you can't."

"I'm sorry, honey," I said. "I have to. Sooner or later, the cops will track you down. You'll go to jail. There will be a trial, and you'll end up on death row. I'm going to save the tax payers some money. And you a lot of grief."

Her mouth spread and tears sprang from her eyes. "I thought…I thought you cared for me."

"If it's any consolation," I said. My throat suddenly felt hot and thick. I didn't trust my voice to finish the sentence, but I did anyway. What came out was hoarse and broken. "If it's any consolation, I care more about you than I've ever cared about a woman before. And this is the hardest thing I've ever done."

"Then don't do it," she said as her tears fell. "I thought we had something."

"You're very sick, Carmen," I said. "I didn't realize how sick until I saw you in that motel room, on the bed with that dead guy. You're unpredictable, which isn't good because you know too much about me. You're very sick, and it's the kind of sickness that can't be cured. I'm putting you down, honey. Like a lame animal, I'm putting you down. I'm sorry, but I can't let you live."

"No!" she screamed, startling me. She dropped to her knees. "I'll do anything, Benedetti, any-anything you want! Anything!

Please don't do this, pluh-please. Kiss me, will you? Please, just kiss me and don't do this, please, I'm begging you, please kiss m—"

Tears stung my eyes as I fired the gun. Even with my blurry vision, I saw the hole appear in her forehead, saw the flash of red spray behind her head. She jerked backward on her knees, then fell to the side.

I went to her and put the gun back under my belt in the small of my back. I picked her up in my arms, went to the side of the grave and leaned forward, let her fall into the hole.

I got the shovel from the rear of the Cayenne and began to scoop the dirt back into the grave. She lay face-up in the bottom of the hole, one arm across her stomach, the other at her side, one leg crossed over the other.

In less than a minute, she was little more than a mound beneath the dirt. Before long, even that was gone.

She was too good to be true, I thought as I went back to the SUV and put my shovel in. I gathered up the picnic, put the basket and blanket into the back of the Cayenne. Too good to be true.

I had to sit at the wheel for a long time before I could drive back home, because I couldn't see. I was blinded by stinging, punishing tears.

About the Author

Ray Garton has been writing novels, novellas, short stories, and essays for more than 30 years. His work spans the genres of horror, crime, suspense, and even comedy. *Live Girls* was nominated for the Bram Stoker Award in 1988, and Garton received the Grand Master of Horror Award at the 2006 World Horror Convention. He lives in northern California with his wife Dawn, where he is at work on a new novel.

BIBLIOGRAPHY

NOVELS AND NOVELLAS

411
Bestial
Biofire
Crawlers
Crucifax
Dark Channel

Darklings
Live Girls
Lot Lizards
Loveless
Night Life
Meds
Murder Was My Alibi
Ravenous
Scissors
Seductions
Serpent Girl
Sex and Violence in Hollywood
Shackled
The Folks
The Folks 2
The Loveliest Dead
The Man in the Palace Theater
The New Neighbor
Trade Secrets
Trailer Park Noir
Vortex

Zombie Love

<u>COLLECTIONS</u>
Methods of Madness
'Nids And Other Stories
Pieces of Hate
Slivers of Bone
The Disappeared and Other Stories
The Girl in the Basement and Other Stories
Wailing and Gnashing of Teeth

Curious about other Crossroad Press books? Stop by our
website: http://crossroadpress.com
We offer quality writing
in digital, audio, and print formats.

Subscribe to our newsletter on the website homepage and
receive a free eBook.